P9-DHZ-095

BENEATH CAAQI'S WINGS

Rich Shapero

BENEATH CAAQI'S WINGS

a novel

HALF MOON BAY, CALIFORNIA

TooFar Media
500 Stone Pine Road, Box 3169
Half Moon Bay, CA 94019

Library of Congress Cataloging-in-Publication Data is available.

ISBN: 978-1-7335259-8-5

Cover artwork by Dean Buchanan
Cover design by Michael Baron Shaw
Artwork copyright © 2021 Rich Shapero

Printed and Bound by CPI Group (UK) Ltd, Croydon, CR0 4YY

26 25 24 23   1 2 3 4 5

1

*S*hrieks rose from the ridge, hovering and peeling, sinking through the boughs of the giant roroas on either side. Midafternoon sun lit the puzzled bark, the winding vines swollen like veins on straining arms. Panting, gasps and guffaws, choked exclamations—

None of the adults approved of the game the boys played, least of all the villa owners. Storm-the-Palace was the name Rangi had given it. In years past, the girls had often been drawn in, but the risks were greater now, the play more perilous. In addition to pushing and shoving, hands became claws and fists that dealt blows. Rather than contending with the boys, the girls watched from a few yards away.

Jema stood beside Kris, pattering while she wove a gold ribbon through the black locks above her best friend's ear.

On the hillock of blocky limestone, the boys were elbowing and butting their way to the top. The outcrop was thirty feet tall and the block sides were shear, so when someone fell, cuts and bruises were likely. Jema looked over her shoulder. No adults in sight. When she turned back, Rangi was rising above the others. A year or two earlier, anyone might have won the scrabble, but that too had changed. The swarthy-skinned native boy, the eldest at sixteen, was always the victor now. In the spring his voice had deepened, and his shoulders were thick and muscled. As Jema watched, Wyatt croaked, waving his arms and losing his footing. Lanky, knees folded, he landed on the earth below, gasping as the visor of the sportsman's cap jumped from his brow. As he lifted himself, Jema saw that his shirt was torn. "He'll get a thrashing for that," she said.

But Kris wasn't listening. Her eyes were fixed on the top of the Palace. Rangi had reached it and stood there now, arms spread, gazing down with lordly terror.

"He's not playing," Kris said, regardful but chafed.

"He's fierce," Jema agreed. "He should give someone else a turn."

She saw Pate rising, approaching the top, kneeing over a block, boosting himself. "Pate's smarter," she murmured. "Patient. Far-seeing."

"Pate lacks cunning," Kris said.

"But he's in control of himself," Jema replied. Like Rangi, Pate was swarthy, of native heritage. The two were brothers of sorts, but different in the way they were emerging as men. "Pate's like a grownup," Jema said.

Kris met her gaze, eyes glittering. "You might be a pair."

Jema laughed, fuddled by the thought. She hugged Kris, who giggled and returned the embrace. This too had changed. As close as they'd been for so many years, the two had grown still closer of late. Their bond had a new foundation: a consuming interest in boys. They were magically, inexplicably drawn, and they both found comfort and reassurance in sharing their feelings and imagining where those feelings might lead.

"Pate won't win," Kris said. "Watch this." And she left Jema's side, hurrying toward the Palace, hair flying. A cheer rose from the girls.

Kris barged through the melee, starting up, shoving boys aside, locked on her target. Pate was rising with his back to her. She came up behind him, gripped his shoulders and sent him tumbling down. Jema moaned for Pate and clapped for her friend.

Rangi faced Kris, snarking his lip, nostrils wide. His full cheeks, bared teeth and fiery temper menaced her. "I don't need your help," he warned. Kris gave a howl and reached for him—playful or trying to pull him down, Jema couldn't tell.

Rangi grunted and drove the heels of his hands at her sternum.

Kris teetered, hunched and came boiling back up, screaming and hurling her fist into Rangi's middle. He fell to his knees, hands down, sucking. Then he stiffened and twisted, striking Kris in the head. She collapsed like a doll stuffed with sawdust, spilling onto her side, rolling down the limestone shelves to the bottom.

Jema saw: Rangi had a rock in his hand.

Two boys cheered, but the hoots of the girls drowned

them out. Jema and the others were hurrying forward. A gash had opened in Kris' brow.

Rangi didn't care. He raised both arms, asserting his triumph.

Jema sank beside Kris, lifting her friend's head. The dark eyes flickered.

Pulling the blouse from her skirt, Jema pressed the cloth to Kris' wound. "What was that?" she shouted at Rangi.

"Don't ruin your shirt," Kris said.

"Bonehead," a girl snarled at Rangi. "It's a game," another assailed him.

"I guess I lost," Kris laughed, trying to raise herself.

Jema helped her up.

Then heads turned and Rangi's father appeared—Hunu the groundskeeper, striding toward them, face stern, with his nappy noggin and grizzled chin.

Hunu approached Kris and reached for her head. He held it in his chapped hands, touching her brow with his thumb, studying the wound with deep concern.

"It's nothing," Kris said.

Pate was by Hunu's elbow, shamefaced. Hunu turned to him. "Take care of her," he ordered.

Then Hunu headed for Rangi. Like a thundercloud rising above the jungle, he mounted the Palace, seized his son with a burly arm and dragged him wailing off the summit, cursing the boy in his native tongue. The two crossed the courtyard, headed toward Hunu's thatched hut.

Pate reached for Kris, but she shook him off. "I said it's

nothing." She turned, following Rangi. "I'm going to kill him," she swore.

Pate raised his brows at Jema.

No matter how angry Kris was, Jema knew, it wouldn't matter. Kris thought about Rangi every waking hour. She went to sleep imagining she was in his arms. Her longing was a kind of furor, a mindless conviction, as if she was halfway to winning the boy with her pain. As if she was almost there.

On the steps of the Palace, boys bereft of their leader made half-hearted swings at each other, unable to duplicate Rangi's fury.

Two other girls were at Kris' hip. "Put a bandage on it," Jema said softly. Kris nodded and strode away.

Jema glanced at Pate and started across the courtyard, headed toward the Governor's villa, wondering if he would follow. He did. Then he moved beside her. The boys were dispersing now, like a school of tadpoles.

"The attraction isn't equal," Pate said.

Jema shook her head. "A rock."

"He can't help himself," Pate said. "He has to win. There's no rule he won't break."

Jema thought about how she might answer, wishing she had Kris' courage. Then, inspired perhaps by Kris' abandon with Rangi, she took a chance.

"You're not that way," she told Pate. And that was true. Though they shared their native heritage, the two boys could not have been more different.

She looked to see how her words had landed, disappointed

when Pate's gaze skittered away. He hadn't taken her words as a compliment. Was he hurt by them?

"Will Hunu beat him?" she asked.

Pate nodded. "He'll be angry with me too."

It was easy for Jema to imagine Pate being regretful or unsure of himself. But she had never seen him discouraged. Unlike the rest of them, he seemed immune to defeat. Being an orphan, she thought, had made him strong. And a little resistant, perhaps, to expressions of affection.

She had always been fond of Pate. They'd been friends since childhood. But her feelings about him were changing. "The attraction wasn't equal," Pate had said. And what about them? Something about Pate drew her. Whatever it was— He was shorter than Rangi, with a keener mind and private eyes. Not like the other boys, dopey and self-centered. But he was so much harder to fathom. I'm the one everyone likes, she reminded herself. But did that matter to Pate? He had a mind of his own.

Pate was watching her, seeing her thoughtfulness.

She smiled, a flash of affection. And then— All at once, she wanted to kiss him. To touch her lips to his for the very first time.

The impulse shocked her. I can be brave, she thought. As brave as Kris. She was attracted to Pate, in a way she'd never felt before. He seemed to understand that. He was raising his hand, perhaps to touch her shoulder. But the hand hesitated, paused in midair and returned to his side.

What did that mean? What should she do? Jema looked

away; then without even thinking, she lowered her hand to his and brushed his fingers.

A moment of great discomfort. When she looked, Pate's head was bowed. Then, as she watched, he turned away. The contact had been brief, almost involuntary. A harmless gesture—

But the mistake had been made.

Jema shivered and drew a breath. A cold breeze passed between them.

The season was changing. In the jungle, it was never as cold as it was in the capital, but you wanted a fire on chilly nights.

"We're loading the grates," Pate said.

Jema stood before the full-length mirror in her room, smoothing the shoulders on a dress made in a foreign land, white with blue piping.

Outside, with the others, things were clouded—doubtful, uncertain. But here, in front of the silvered glass, everything was as clear as could be. The reflection revealed her true nature. And Jema liked what she saw.

Good fortune had blessed her with taste and a copious wardrobe, but her real advantage was the sparkling personality that winked through her poise and gestures and her shifting expressions. Only Kris saw all of her. But everyone whose eyes fell upon her found themselves smiling. At fifteen years, her manner was coy and enticing. Her hair was fine and scarfy, and silvery blond, and when she guided it over her shoulder—as she did now—it caught people's eyes. She was special, they all could see that. They didn't need to speak to her—from a distance, they knew. Jema communed with her reflection, play-acting, posing, trying on one look after another, assuring herself that she was, indeed, unique. And the disappointment with Pate faded.

She turned from the mirror, passed through the French doors and stepped out onto the Flying Terrace, gazing at the settlement, set like a jewel on the ridge, with the jungle around it. On either side, the greenery sloped steeply down, tangled and thick. One side faced the capital, impossibly distant. The other side faced the native lands, a wilderness that for generations had protected settlers from the warring tribes.

The settlement's two villas, of similar design, faced each other across the courtyard, with the huts, shelters and outbuildings crowded at the wings' extremities. The dwarf rail line, like a wayward liana, wound from a wood lot, past the livestock pens, around the orchard and gardens, with a loop that ran for miles through the jungle on the native side of the ridge. Jema and her parents called their villa "home" every summer, and Kris and her parents did the same.

The Chancellor and the Governor had been friends and political allies before the girls were born. They'd purchased the property together, for themselves and their wives, during their rise to power. Every summer, as heat descended on the capital, the men handed their authority to deputies and retreated to their private world, forgetting the duties of state for a while. When they were young, the girls had argued about which was more powerful. Kris contended that her father, as Chancellor, was a national leader; Jema argued that the Chancellor was appointed, while the Governor of the largest province was elected and had a mandate from the people.

It was just youthful quibbling. On the estate all the men were important, and the women too; every summer, the pieces fit together. Some were employed full time, others were only with them during the holiday. The class distinctions that prevailed in the capital were ignored, and all were treated as equals. For the solstice, Kris' mother hosted the annual garden party, which the residents greatly enjoyed.

But the holiday spirit had ended three months before. Unrest in the capital protracted their summer stay, and then a smoldering insurrection had forced the two leaders and their wives to return, along with some of the staff. Men cleared the overgrown trail for the horses and wagons, hacking vines and branches with machetes, building rafts to ford the rivers, and the caravan departed. Fourteen children and a dozen adults remained. During the month now passed, there had been no communication. The Governor's words still echoed in Jema's ears. "You'll be safer here." How close to the conflict were they? Had they been taken captive? Were they even alive?

She descended the tiled stair, seeing Kris crossing the courtyard from the Chancellor's villa. Jema spent her evenings there, in her friend's home. "Don't worry" was the last thing Jema's mother had said.

At the bottom of the stair, she took a floret of rata blooms from the vase and snapped the long stem off.

Jema met Kris on the outdoor walkway. Her forehead was bandaged, and the flesh around it was rosy and puffed. "I love that dress," Jema said, placing the rata stem behind Kris' ear so the spray hid the bandage.

"I should know better," Kris laughed and took Jema's hand.

The two girls started down the colonnade together.

"A hundred years ago," Kris said, "his relatives were eating each other."

"I walked back to the villa with Pate," Jema told her.

"He really likes you."

"I'm not sure," Jema shared her doubt. "Maybe a little."

"A lot," Kris said. "He's just shy. In a good way, not like Rangi."

"I can't tell what he's thinking."

"Do you want him to kiss you?" Kris asked.

Jema laughed and nodded.

"Put your lips close to his," Kris said, making a spout of her mouth. "If he asks if he can, say 'yes.' He might not ask. He might just do it."

Kris slowed and stopped. She looked around them and lowered her voice. "When people kiss, sometimes they play with each other's tongues. I've been reading about it in one of mother's books."

Jema stared at her, and Kris stared back.

"I'm going to do that," Kris said.

"I am too," Jema agreed. They said things to each other they wouldn't say to anyone else.

"Boys don't know a thing about love," Kris said. "It's up to us. We have to get them going. Kissing is just the beginning." Her eyes glinted like the Governor's razor. "If you let Pate kiss you, he'll want more."

"I'm not ready for that," Jema said.

"I am," Kris replied.

Hurried steps sounded behind them, and a voice called out. They turned to see Ry-Lynn approaching. A big girl of fourteen years, with sandy hair and a triangle chin.

"It's your best friend," Kris smirked.

Ry-Lynn waved some papers before her. She wanted to be close to Jema and often imagined she was.

"Look," Ry-Lynn exclaimed, wiggling in front of Kris, presenting the papers to Jema. "Answers to next week's test," she beamed. "Wyatt copied them for me."

Jema returned the smile. Wyatt's mother was their teacher. Wyatt, it seemed, had succumbed to Ry-Lynn's requests.

"He's very upset," Ry-Lynn laughed. "He's such a good boy."

"Thanks," Jema said.

"History," Kris sneered.

Ry-Lynn folded the papers and put them in the placket pocket of Jema's dress. Then she stepped aside, and Jema and Kris continued down the colonnade.

The boys' shouts reached them from the woodland beyond, with Rangi's foremost. Whatever punishment he'd received was behind him.

As they approached a vine-covered outbuilding, a small fist knocked on the window. "Keep walking," Kris said.

Jema saw Melody through the pane, her nose pressed to the glass. "Jema, Jema," the little girl cried. Jema halted.

Mr. Trett, Melody's father, appeared behind her and raised the sash. The estate manager was a calm bald man who knew the ways of adults, in addition to the workings of water pumps and boilers, the tallies of foods and supplies, and the logic of all things mechanical and precise. It was a marvel to Jema that Mr. Trett could bear the burden of domestic order for so many. Before the Governor and Chancellor departed, they'd given him full charge.

Melody reached her arms out. "Can I come?"

Kris shook her head.

"Of course," Jema said. The little girl had an Asian look, with black hair and secluded eyes. She was five, liked to feed the lambs in the paddock and take care of her doll, and she craved time with the older girls. Jema circled her waist and pulled her through the window.

"It's not your responsibility," Mr. Trett said. But Melody was an only child, the youngest on the estate; and Mrs. Trett, being the Chancellor's assistant, had left with the caravan. In the office with her father, Melody was a constant distraction.

"I'm going to see Hunu and Caaqi," Jema told her.

Kris groaned.

"I want to pet him," Melody said.

"You're coming with me." And Kris led her away.

When Jema arrived at Hunu's hut, Pate was straddling the weathered bench, chopping wood with a hand ax. He paused, and for a moment she was startled by his look, deep and private, only for her. She allowed herself to bask in his attention, letting him see how glad it made her. Was he sorry he'd recoiled when she'd touched his hand? Jema turned her head.

Hunu was cutting up fruit with an oversize blade. He was wrinkled and graying but still very strong. She could see the tautness in his neck and the force in his strokes. There was a bucket of nuts on the ground by his boot.

As she approached, Hunu lowered the large blade.

"I fished this out of my trunk this morning," he said. "I thought, 'It was made to be used.'"

Jema could tell he was wading into one of his stories.

"It's a spearhead," Pate said, stepping beside her. "It belonged to a chief."

"One of my kin." Hunu motioned Jema closer, kneeling and turning the blade.

It was tarnished, mottled with circlets and trimmed with a silver edge.

"He used it in the tribal wars," Hunu said.

"Cannibal wars," Pate nodded.

The island's native history, and the legacy of cannibalism,

had exerted its fear and fascination on Jema from an early age. The stories raised questions about the human family, about reckless and bloody impulses that had threatened once and might threaten again. Matters that shouldn't be forgotten, puzzles that must be solved.

Hunu's brow rumpled. "At dawn, the chief wakes them. 'Start up your ovens, boys. We've a long day ahead.' When a warrior falls, they hack him to pieces and have him for lunch. Then they return to battle." He saw Jema's reaction and laughed.

She laughed back. Pate touched the blade.

There was something about Hunu and his stories that made it easy for them to be together. Jema wished it was like that when she and Pate were alone.

"It speared men," Hunu said, "and eels too. The chief had a taste for both, so they mingled the meats and baked them together. It remembers." He put his thumb to the silver edge and closed his eyes, as if the blade had its own desires and he could discern them. "It's not living now," he said. "But once it was."

Hunu loved the past, and so did Pate—not the pale history that Wyatt's mom taught—but the past that was part of the jungle, dense and lush and wet, where light rarely reached the forest floor; magic was everywhere, everything had an attraction or repulsion to everything else; a delicious place, but terrible too; a place where people might go mad, reverting to a savagery they had never successfully shed.

Pate didn't know who his father was. Hunu had adopted him and raised him and his true son, Rangi, on stories about their native past. The other kids ignored the old man, but Jema found him endlessly interesting. From the Flying Terrace, she would watch him grooming the light-splashed arbors, repairing fences, oiling the axles of the Royal Express, knowing that he carried the jungle inside him, wondering what part of the magical realm he would unfold next. War camps and shelters, grisly middens, rings and pits for divine frenzies and ritual beheadings— No one knew the full extent of the island's mysteries, Hunu said, its haunted recesses, its undreamt-of creatures— The jungle's far reaches were still unexplored.

Caaqi shrieked.

"I think our bird's hungry," Hunu said.

He nodded, set the spearhead aside and rose. The old man circled the hut and loosed the latch of an open-air shed. When he returned, he was holding a large wooden cage before him. Through the bars, Jema could see the wild parrot gripping the gnarled branch it used as a perch.

The bird stooped his head, as if peering at her beneath some barrier. He was fourteen inches in height and his chest, like his back, was lapped with chocolate scallops. When he unfolded himself—as he did now—his underside was woven like a basket with scarlet and gold. He threw his head back, fanning his tail and spreading his wings.

"Caaqi," he rasped, with a voice like Hunu's.

Jema clapped her hands. Pate laughed. The bird's black eye gleamed.

Every summer, like all the kids, she'd heard parrots calling from the jungle, and from time to time she'd spotted one winging through the crowns of the trees. But she'd never seen one up close. A month before, the day after her parents left with the caravan, Hunu had found the wounded bird in the woods, in a net of emerald ferns. One of Caaqi's wings was bloody and limp. Hunu built the cage, and they'd nursed him back to health. Jema came every day to help, and the visits seemed to fill the void of her parents' absence, along with bringing her closer to Pate.

"Tribute," Hunu said, nodding at the fruit board and the bucket of nuts.

Pate grabbed the offerings. Jema crept forward till her face was a foot from the bars. Caaqi's claws were the color of bone. His eye was a convex night with a geometry of stars, and as she watched, rays flashed and speared, connecting the stars to each other.

Pate pushed cracked nuts through the bars. Caaqi hopped down from his perch and retrieved one with his claw. He lifted the shell, toes on either side, like the Governor holding a goblet.

"His wing's healed," Hunu said. "He's ready."

Caaqi peered over his goblet at Jema. "Ready," he rasped. Then he pecked the shell, removing the lobes of nut.

Hanging from the peak of the cage, Jema saw, was a large

magenta flower shaped like a trumpet, its flared mouth down. It had a powerful fragrance.

Hunu touched the flower's stalk. "The tribes called this Caaqi's Breath. It's always in bloom."

"Even in the winter?" Jema asked.

Hunu nodded. "The trick is finding them. I came across it in the forest this morning. It's a sign."

"Of what?"

"It's time to release him," Hunu said.

Jema wasn't sure what that would mean for her and Pate. The parrot seemed woven into the new magnetism between them.

"Caaqi won't forget us," Hunu told her. "He knows who we are. He has many ways to reach us. When your thoughts are drifting, he might land on your shoulder. When you're asleep, he might fly through your dream. When you're in the forest, he might emerge from a cloud of Caaqi's Breath pollen."

Jema could see the golden powder on the trumpet's anther. She imagined a billow of glowing dust filling the air, sifting around her.

"Caaqi brings change," Hunu said. "That's what they thought. Some find victory. Some find love. Some lose their senses."

The language Hunu used was turning the parrot into a creature of fable. Caaqi's head turned down, accepting the role it seemed. Jema imagined his proud silhouette plummeting through the roroa boughs, underwings flashing, batting and cupping as he called her name. The silhouette reached with its claws and settled on her arm.

"Master of the past," Hunu said. "A fiery protector. Author of love and bloodshed—the things that frighten us most."

I'm not frightened of love, Jema thought. And then—

A rasping scream made her jump.

Caaqi's head had turned. He was staring at her single-eyed. Between the bright spokes, stars pricked and glittered, a cruel hunger fixed on her with such force that she felt herself falling and reached out her hand. Then, as quickly, the fierce zodiac was drowned in black, and Caaqi was just a parrot again.

Jema picked up a wedge of fruit, licked the juice that ran down her wrist and pushed the wedge between the bars. Caaqi took it, crushing, swallowing.

The parrot blinked, gripped his perch and rocked forward, clicking his beak. Was he about to say something?

"The cage is a jail to him," Pate said.

"You can't keep parrots long," Hunu agreed.

For a moment, Jema thought he'd said "parents."

Footsteps were crunching the gravel. Jema met Pate's eyes, but she couldn't tell what was behind them. Pate turned and she followed his gaze.

Rangi appeared on the path, swung the gate back and strode toward them, swatting bugs, sweating and wiping his brow with his shirt.

"Cannibal tales?" he said with a note of scorn.

Jema saw Hunu's expression sour.

"I love them," she said, speaking loudly enough for the graying father to hear.

Rangi rolled his eyes. "He makes them up while he's trimming your hedge."

Hunu faced his son, wincing, feeling an old wound. "Don't you have something to tend to?"

Caaqi seemed engaged with the conflict, edging closer on his perch, tilting his head toward Rangi in what seemed a gesture of encouragement.

Jema looked at Hunu, but the groundskeeper had already lifted the cage and turned, starting back to the shed.

That night, the two girls dropped off quickly. Kris was a sound sleeper—the rigors of being Kris demanded relief. Jema woke before dawn beside her best friend, with a strange feeling. She'd emerged from a dream both alarming and rapturous. She was standing in a clearing surrounded by giant trees, a place of foresight and magic, alone in the darkness. Her child's self was dribbling out of her middle and down her front, soaking into the jungle floor. And as that familiar self disappeared, in its place, a newer, more exciting self lifted up, fountaining into her body, glittering in every corner. This luminous self was someone she barely knew.

Jema rose and put on her clothes. She could smell the sweet odor of roroa, and as she passed the leaded windows, she saw flames in the fireplace. With the first chill of fall, they'd let it burn all night. She left the Chancellor's villa quietly, found her way along the hedges to the low stone wall and opened the gate. The sky was thick with stars, and the winking lights prickled her arms.

Hunu's hut came into view. She approached it with soft steps, imagining the old man and the two native boys asleep inside. When she reached the shed, she touched the door, opening it slowly.

The fragrance of the trumpet reached her. She could see the ghostly bloom at the top of the cage. The scent was so fresh and potent, it seemed to bear you away—to some other time, some other place. Was this how you felt when the golden pollen of Caaqi's Breath was sifting around you?

She could hear the parrot rustling. He knows I'm here, she thought.

"Caaqi?" she whispered, rounding the cage.

A starlit eye blinked from the gloom.

Why had he fallen from the sky, she wondered. And why so close to her villa? Did he have some purpose? Was he there for a reason?

A fiery protector. Author of love and bloodshed. Could he read her mind? Could he feel her secret desires?

If Caaqi had some understanding of the new self releasing inside her, perhaps he had come to father her future, to do what the Governor had done for his little girl.

A laugh left her lips. What was she thinking?

Jema stood in the darkness eyeing the bird's silhouette—his feathered crown and his crescent beak.

After a time she retreated, returning the way she had come, though she didn't feel at all like the person who had passed that way a short while before.

At dawn, before Kris and the others were stirring, Jema crossed the courtyard, entered her villa and found her way to the Governor's study. The shelves on all sides were loaded with books, many first editions signed by the authors. The books always gave her comfort, as she felt her father's presence among them. Some who addressed him by his title thought him teachy, so when she called him "Governor" it amused them both.

She pulled one of his favorites from the shelf, sat in her father's chair and began to read. An hour later, sunlight appeared in the transom window and she hurried upstairs, recalling it wasn't a school day. After washing she selected a dress of green chiffon, and when it was on, she turned in front of the mirror thinking of Kris, wanting to share the strange dream with her. The dream and her encounter with Caaqi.

She found Kris and the girls at the table in the coppice, sitting in the shade, jabbering while they thumbed through a half-dozen magazines taken by Kris from her mother's closet. Jema started toward her, but Kris was immersed, so when Ry-Lynn waved, Jema sat on the bench beside her.

"I love you in green," Ry-Lynn said, smoothing Jema's collar.

Jema smiled and sniffed the air. "Limes," she guessed. Ry-Lynn was a medley of scents—berries and plums one day, citrus the next—whatever was ripe in the orchards tended by her mother. Finger, Ry-Lynn's kid brother, tugged her dress and moaned. He was too young to play with the boys. Ry-Lynn tousled his hair. "Go sit by the tree."

"I want to look like her," Dee said, pointing at an open magazine.

"You already do," Ry-Lynn observed.

Dee was thin as a sapling. Once shy and demure, something had happened that summer. On her fourteenth birthday, she was overcome by self-loathing. Dee was starving herself.

"This one looks like your mom," Venus said, smiling at Jema.

"She does," Jema agreed. "I like her necklace."

"She went crazy," Kris said. "She died in a sanitarium."

Venus sighed, as if the sad end was her own.

She's carrying such a heavy load, Jema thought. Poor Venus wished she was tall, but she was short and pudgy. She had a pug nose, which she wished was pointy. And being eleven, she wished she was older. When she ate something sweet, she wished she could stop. She wished she had Dee's discipline and Kris' grit. By the time she reached Jema's age, Venus had told her, she hoped her failings would be behind her.

Jema rose, looking to Kris, wanting to call her aside. But her friend was absorbed by the images on the well-worn pages. Glamorous and coy, frozen in youth, dazzled by sun and floodlight. Could your life be that full, your waist that small?

Kris was as blinded by hope as any of them. Jema recalled her dream, doubting that Kris would understand.

She turned, stepped toward the tree and sat down beside Finger.

He snuffled, squirming closer, leaning his head against her shoulder.

"Give it time," Jema said.

The children gathered in the Chancellor's villa for lunch and again for dinner, summoned by the clanging of the cook's copper bell. Pate missed both meals. Jema heard he was in the woods with Hunu felling trees, so when dinner ended, she followed the narrow-gauge rails away from the settlement, listening for the loco. Its rumble and squeal had a home in her heart.

The Governor, whose love of trains dated back to his boyhood, had built the dwarf rail system for his own entertainment. He would dress in outdated garb and play engineer, one hand sounding the whistle, the other on the throttle, pulling a single passenger car. Over time as more track was laid, he thought the Royal Express could have practical utility, so three flat cars were added and a long loop was laid into the unlogged native jungle.

Jema heard the chugging and the little loco appeared, sparking and creaking, cab red, roof green, rounding a curve. She could see Hunu through the glass and Pate beside him, feeding wood to the boiler. On the first flat car, logs were piled. As the loco reached her, Hunu waved and Pate jumped from the cab, landing on the rail bed and skipping up beside her. The second flat car passed, and Jema saw the carcasses of lambs recently slaughtered. They still had their fleece, and their heads were turned, so their fate wasn't obvious. They might have been enjoying the ride.

A sweet perfume reached her, the sun on young wool, and then the resin scent of hewn logs on the third flat car as it passed. An odor of grease and boiler smoke rose from Pate's dungarees. The dream of a new self seemed to have sharpened her senses.

The train vanished around the bend, and its sounds faded. They followed the tracks, walking in silence. There wasn't much space between them, but Jema felt it keenly. She longed to take Pate's hand. Twilight was settling over the woodland on either side. A small hedge of luminescent maruna began to glow.

They reached the depot, crossed the courtyard and entered the Great Room of the Governor's villa. A few of the kids were mingling there, as they often did at the end of the day. When Rodney saw Jema, he approached with Snugg beside him. The two boys were best friends and an unlikely pairing: Rodney immense and powerful for his fifteen years, while Snugg was delicate, almost elfin.

"The fire's dying," Rodney complained. "Snugg is cold."

Jema laughed. "You might have added some wood."

On the stone apron of the fireplace, there were sections

of log and a hatchet and splitting stump. Pate set to work, and the wood flew apart, clattering on the stones, the bright salmon-orange of the roroa laid bare.

Jema retrieved the fly-aways, filling her arms and setting them on the scorched apron. In the throat of the fireplace, a gray mound of ashes was still smoking, sending tendrils into the blackened flu.

It happened quickly, like a trap being sprung. Pate tipped the split logs together, leaned forward and blew on the ash at the center.

Jema heard an explosive *pop*, felt a searing heat as the fireball bloomed and the eruption rose. It seemed to rush through her, as if she and Pate were the wood, and the fire was pulling them with it, through the dark tunnel and into sky.

Creosote came loose, crashing onto the grate, flaming gold, tumbling over the apron and the parquet floor.

Pate's eyes flared, reflecting the glow. "Leave," he muttered, and then he was shouting, "Get out, get out." But his words were masked by the roar of the venting.

Jema grabbed Rodney's shoulder and Snugg's hand. "Fire," she cried, and the kids in the Great Room bolted as one through the giant doors chanting, "Fire, fire!"

Outside the villa, Pate scanned the courtyard. Jema saw grownups emerging from huts and outbuildings in response to the cries.

"We need Hunu," Pate said.

She turned to look. The air above the villa chimney was blurred and smoky.

Could it be stopped? Wyatt's dad appeared, hurrying forward, waving his hands. Then Mr. Trett with Melody in his arms, and Hunu barking orders and pointing.

Where the chimney emerged from the roof, Jema saw, the mossy shingles were steaming. Low flames appeared, attacking the bricks—the channel that had imprisoned them for so many years.

Wyatt's dad was unspooling hoses. Others clanged forward, arms full of buckets. Mr. Trett sputtered self-accusingly: the chimney hadn't been properly cleaned that fall. The adults were in motion; but the fire, it seemed to Jema, was moving much faster.

The roof flames rose. Spirals of sparks were caught by the breeze and scattered downwind, some falling on the arbors and winking out, others landing on thatched roofs and limestone tiles.

Through the melee, Jema saw the hut where Ry-Lynn lived burst into flames. The children were gathered now in the courtyard before the Governor's villa, watching. Dread appeared on Pate's face and horror on Snugg's.

A line of adults formed, and they began passing buckets of water to each other. Rangi waved his arm to the boys. "Come on," he shouted, but none moved to help.

Mr. Trett lurched toward them with Melody on his hip, looking for the first time like he was not in control. He thrust Melody into Jema's arms. "My doll, my doll," the child cried. "We'll find it," Jema assured her. The air around them was thick with smoke.

"All of you," Mr. Trett ordered the children, "into the coach house."

Why there? Jema thought.

"We can carry buckets," Rangi protested.

"You're coming with me," Mr. Trett barked.

He led them at a run, yelling and herding the group toward the small stone building, and when he reached it, he slid open the metal door and motioned them in.

"Stay here. Don't leave," he directed. Venus was wide-eyed, gazing numbly at the mowers, shovels and rakes. "Understand?" Mr. Trett pointed at Kris, giving her the fault if any disobeyed. "I'll be back," he told them. Melody's cries rose to a siren-howl as he closed the door.

Jema scanned the group, counting heads. All fourteen of them were there.

Rangi sat on a harrow. Finger knelt by his shin. "They treat us like babies," Rangi grumbled. "No one lets me do anything," Finger said.

The coach house had two dusty windows. Kris, Jema and a couple of the girls crowded around one. Melody was shaking in Jema's arms, tears washing her cheeks. The adults were carrying a ladder and a big canvas.

"What are they doing?" Kris wondered.

Pate came up behind them. "Trying to choke the fire," he guessed, peering through the window.

"We could be helping," Rangi growled. He was up now, headed toward the other window. "That won't work," he said, looking out. "They're too late."

Maybe he's right, Jema thought. The Great Room was on fire. There were flames in the windows.

"You don't know," Wyatt said, swinging away from the glass, pulling his visor down.

Kris gripped Jema's shoulder. "He's climbing the ladder."

When Jema turned back, she could see Hunu halfway up it with the canvas over his shoulder. Another man was behind him trying to help, wrestling with the load.

"That's my dad," Ry-Lynn said with a tremulous voice. "My dad's with him."

Jema could see the two men mounting the eaves near the flaming chimney. Pate had fallen silent, watching with a new apprehension.

"The roof's on fire," Rodney mumbled in disbelief.

Hunu stood on it now, crossing the blazing shingles, as sure as he was when he padded through the garden, a profusion of flames growing around him.

The roof was burning, Jema thought, and the two men were adding their weight to it. She could see them approach the chimney, struggle to open the canvas, each gripping a corner like two women hanging laundry out to dry.

Rangi had bowed his head. Jema saw him raise a trembling hand and put it over his eyes. Despite the contempt and resentment, Hunu was his father.

As she turned back, the wind snapped the canvas away. Then the unbelievable happened: the burning circle of roof around the chimney, on which the two men stood, collapsed. Ry-Lynn's dad was sucked into the hole. Hunu clung, swinging in the gap, arms burning, his hair and face too. A breathless moment, then his grip gave and he sank into the blaze.

It was like a hole had opened inside her. Jema felt Pate shudder, and she moved closer, hugging Melody tightly, the warmth of the little girl's body between them. Caught in her own shock at Hunu's loss, she could barely imagine Pate's and was unprepared when she felt his arm circling her waist. *He needs me*, she thought.

Ry-Lynn faced the window, eyes wide. Her mouth opened, but no sound emerged. Rangi turned away, stepping to a dark corner, like a child who'd been reprimanded.

"What happened?" Finger asked.

Outside, the roof of the villa continued to collapse, triggering explosions that sent glowing detritus in every direction. The thatch of the schoolroom was burning. The roofs of other cottages glittered with embers and tufts of fire.

Pate raised his head. Jema saw him face Rangi, and their eyes met. For a moment, the rivalry seemed to dissolve. Then Pate's nose twitched.

He turned, searching, fixing on the near window's corner. Hay stacked against the outside wall of the coach house was smoking, and the smoke was seeping through the jamb and beneath the door, collecting around their feet.

"We've got to get out of here," Pate said.

Rangi straightened, nodding. Venus coughed. As the kids watched, the smoke rose to their knees. Kris stepped toward Rangi. He strode to the coach house door and slid it open.

Snugg looked alarmed. "Mr. Trett said—"

"Forget that," Rangi snarled, grabbing Kris by the arm. Ry-Lynn was sobbing. "What happened?" Finger insisted.

Pate urged Jema toward the door. For a moment, she imagined the Governor had paused and looked south, seeing the smoke leagues away.

Snugg was coughing, and Wyatt and Venus, and Rodney too.

"Hold hands." Pate spoke calmly, as if panic would use the last of their air. He clasped Jema's hand. She took Ry-Lynn's, and Ry-Lynn took Finger's. "Don't let go," Pate said.

"Follow me." Rangi reached for Kris, got hold of her wrist and dragged her through the opening. The others followed, hands linked.

Outside, breathing was easier, but what Jema saw was so much worse. Flames were everywhere. Most of the huts and cottages were burning. Through a drifting smudge, she caught sight of her home. The upper story was a snapping inferno, and the lower was curtained with scarlet and gold.

Rangi led them across the moss-mortared pavers to the slanted door of an underground cellar. But the door was padlocked. The smoke was swirling, embers falling through it. Pate shouted to Rangi and pointed. "The train." The two turned together. The Royal Express car wasn't made of wood, Jema thought. And the depot was brick, with a rocky barricade around it.

Rangi nodded and waved to the others, and they started for the train. Melody's face was soot-stained and striped with tears. She couldn't stop crying. Jema held tight to Ry-Lynn, and behind Ry-Lynn was Finger. Suddenly, with a poignance that would haunt them later, Finger yowled like he was wasp-stung and shouted, "They need our help." He tore free of his sister and raced back across the courtyard.

Ry-Lynn whirled and went running after him, and Jema followed, holding Melody close. Glimpses of Finger came and went as smoke from the burning villa roiled over the court-yard. Were others behind them? Jema couldn't tell. Finger disappeared in the smoke. Melody began to cough, and then Jema did too, but she continued forward, eyes streaming. She lost sight of Ry-Lynn, then stumbled over her, huddled on the ground, choking and struggling for breath. Jema, cradling Melody, tried to help Ry-Lynn up, and then Pate grabbed them both, hurrying them back across the courtyard, toward the train and safety.

Wyatt emerged from the smoke and reached for Ry-Lynn. "The grownups will find him," Wyatt told her. The chain of kids was moving again, blundering through the smoke like a blind worm. Jema was breathless, but Pate was pulling her. They crossed the railroad tracks.

Rangi reached the Royal Express and opened the door of the passenger car. He and Pate urged the others in, helping the smaller ones up the steps. Jema climbed aboard with Melody in her arms. She collapsed in a seat, and a few moments later Pate sank beside her. When the others had boarded, Rangi joined them and closed the door.

Jema drew deep breaths, trying to calm herself, looking

around. The fanciful decor was jarring—the brass fittings, blue velvet curtains and upholstery woven with lianas and ferns. Many birthdays had been celebrated here, with cake and punch for the kids in the moving car, while the Governor manned the loco.

Whimpers, coughing, sighs of relief— Then they crowded the windows.

The settlement was a bowl of fire. Nothing else moved; no man or woman, no child or animal—only leaping flames and boiling smoke. The blaze was consuming Hunu's hut, Jema saw.

Rangi was counting—eleven, twelve, thirteen. A kind of responsibility had descended on him. Jema saw it, and the others did too. Despite his swagger and malice, he was a leader.

"We're all here except Finger," Rangi said.

Ry-Lynn sobbed, "I should have hung on to him."

Rangi collapsed on a seat by himself.

Kris was still standing. Jema looked at her. "I need to be with Pate."

Kris nodded. "I'll bunk with Ry-Lynn."

"I'm hungry," Venus whined. Dee squeezed the younger girl's shoulder. "You can be with me," Dee said, lowering herself. Her slight body took little space on the seat.

Through the window, fire lit the darkness. Ash was falling like snow. The night, Jema knew, would be cold and they had no blankets. Pate rested his head on her shoulder, and a few minutes later, he'd closed his eyes. He seemed restless at first, adjusting and twisting. Was he as troubled as she was, thinking about the fire they'd birthed and the deaths it had caused? She stroked his hair, and his agitation seemed to subside.

What were the grownups doing, she worried. She would never see Hunu again, or his hut, or the parrot he had meant to release—

Melody squirmed in her lap for a while longer, then she too was calm. Finally Jema closed her eyes. Respite came quickly. Lulled by the crackling of flames and the thud of timbers, she slept like she was under a spell.

A dream— Jema entered it running, as Finger had run into the burning. A dream of the past, of a paradise forgotten, revived and returning. Her father was in the Great Room, her mother in bed; and in the study she was curled in the Governor's chair, thumbing the pages of a first edition. Hours came and went, days and years—

Was she still dreaming, or had she emerged from sleep? Jema felt or heard something that caused her to wake, or imagine she had. She raised her shoulders and parted her lids, or imagined she did. She turned and peered through the Express car window and saw something that couldn't have been real.

Amid the shifting tapers of flame, giant columns of smoke were rising, thick and dark, like the bars of a cage. And in the sky above, a great winged creature was soaring, finally set free. His wings were wide, with chocolate feathers and ragged edges. As they batted, they flattened the petering blazes, but the Great Caaqi paid no mind. He cared nothing for the Governor's villa or what remained.

Jema saw the great parrot's head and his crescent beak. The black in his eyes dissolved, showing her his excitement and pride. It was as if he knew some wish of hers, some secret desire that not even she was aware of. That's why he'd come. That's why Caaqi was here.

He tilted his wings, he lowered his head, gliding toward her.

Closer and closer— Until his looming sucked the breath from her lungs, until his furious wings rocked the car, until the scream in his throat drowned her own.

Caaqi's cryptic eye blackened the glass and Jema sank down.

Much later, in the hour before dawn, she could hear a steady rain falling.

To Jema, still half asleep, the rain brought peace. Caaqi had passed. The burning was over. With a power gentle but conclusive, the water's long diagonals cleared the smoke and silenced the hissing remains.

2

The windows of the train car were fogged and glowing with pink light. The drumming of the rain had ended. Jema raised herself, feeling the weight of Melody's shoulders on her middle. Pate was huddled beside her, eyes closed but stirring. In the night, his hand had fallen on her breast. Jema lifted it off and smoothed her front.

Other eyes opened. Snugg, Ry-Lynn. Dee looked gaunt and unrested. The thirteen were stretching and straightening, staring wordlessly at each other.

Rangi twisted his head on his neck. Jema looked at the door of the car, remembering him closing it. The grownups don't know we're here, she thought. Wyatt blinked at her beneath his visor. Rodney frowned. Jema worried about the adults. Had they found an unburnt roof to bed down beneath? Or sought shelter in the forest?

Melody raised her head. "I'm hungry."

Mr. Trett, Jema thought, would be worried about his daughter.

The passenger car was brimming with silent dread and speculation. The enormity of what had happened was too much for any of them.

Rangi swore and stood. "Let's have a look."

He marched to the door and opened it. Feeling the nudge of cold air, Jema helped Melody to her feet. Then Pate and the others stood as one and filed out of the car.

On the ground was a windrow of soot and ash that the rain had washed from the car's roof. Rangi led the group past the loco and across the tracks. Before them, the sun was rising over a steaming ruin. The summer estate was a blackened crater, with the charred remains of the villas on either side. Amid heaps of timber, roof spans and scorched plaster, a mangled passage or a crumbling wall appeared. The outbuildings were blasted caves, puddles and pyres of smoldering ash between.

Kris scanned the ruins. Jema could see the fear in her eyes. There were no adults in sight.

"They're looking for us," Venus said.

Wyatt turned, and so did Ry-Lynn, gazing at the vestiges of their homes.

"We're safe," Rangi bellowed. "We're here." He listened for a response.

No one answered.

"Wake up, will you," Rangi demanded.

No movement in the courtyard or at the jungle borders, no movement in the smoky waste. The char was so bright after the night's rain, it looked painted with black lacquer.

"Please," Snugg cried out.

"Father?" Wyatt swept the smoking grounds.

Jema thought of her parents, in the capital or wherever they might be. They would have no way of knowing what happened. Rangi was striding toward the remains of the Governor's villa. She followed, and so did Pate, with Melody between them. The others were moving too.

When Rangi reached the portico, he stopped. All that remained was the stony threshold. You could see through the villa now—pillars of blasted brick, knee-high vestiges of interior walls. The stair leading up to the second floor was intact, but everything around it was gone. Beyond the blackened spars, the forest was visible, as green as ever.

Pate was peering at her. Jema met his gaze. They had started the fire, she thought. And the blaze had destroyed the Governor's dream, a paradise for them all—destroyed his dream and released a fury no one could control.

The image of Caaqi returned, flying over her burning home, great wings fanning. What was the parrot now but a looming sense of misfortune?

Rangi backed up, grabbed a charred timber and thrust it into the smoking rubble by the villa entry. He dug for a moment, then raised his head and ordered others to follow his lead. Pate nodded to Jema and stooped for a beam. He seemed to understand what Rangi was doing. Jema let go of Melody's hand and found a timber for herself. Others stepped forward—Kris and Dee, Rodney and Snugg.

As Jema shifted a crumbling rafter, exposing live coals, she remembered Hunu and Ry-Lynn's dad on the roof. The grownups had gathered here to help the two men. Ten feet away Rangi grunted, lifting a short span of rail and two steps of a ladder. Pate and Ry-Lynn, Snugg and Wyatt—they were all digging now, pushing charred wood and burnt plaster aside. Rangi seemed fiercely determined. Then he shrank back.

"Corpses," he said.

The word shook Jema. She followed his gaze.

Arms, a leg, Mr. Trett's face, blackened and torn.

"Don't let her see," Pate hissed.

Jema hurried to lead Melody away, while Pate made herding motions to Kris. She responded, turning Venus aside.

A dozen retreating steps and Jema looked back in time to hear Rodney shout. Snugg was holding in both arms what appeared to be a dressmaker's blackened dummy. The sight bristled the hairs on Jema's neck. The dummy's head had hanks of blonde hair—Snugg was holding his mother.

Rodney hurried toward him. Snugg seemed not to see him or anyone else. He was dragging the dummy, stumbling, sobbing and incoherent. Only after he'd fallen did he loose his hold. He jumped up, slapping his smoldering pants and howling while his mother's body smoked in a wallow of charred debris.

Others were stepping forward, calling for their parents as if they might be roused. Dee staggered among the steaming pyres. Wyatt tightroped over a ruck of beams. A grim chorus rose as one after another discovered a body or a blackened limb.

It was clear now what had happened. Beneath the remains of the Flying Terrace lay the grownups' crushed bodies. When it collapsed, it had buried them all.

Pate lifted his timber. "Finger's here," he said softly, eyeing Ry-Lynn. "He was trying to save your father." Pate's voice was steady. Once-orphaned already, he seemed immune to feeling the same grief as the others.

With a choked sob, Ry-Lynn hid her face. Bones, cooked flesh, charred skulls— For Jema, the calamity was inconceivable. Had they all perished on the threshold of her home?

Dee was given the task of tending to Melody, Venus and Snugg, at a good distance. Rangi ordered the rest of them to carry the remains, like blackened firewood, to a garden at the courtyard's edge. There was shock and revulsion, weeping and muzzled terror. Pate did what he could to keep them calm. Jema, despite her horror, bore her share.

The baked limbs and body parts were light and odorless. A surprise, how easy it was to lift and carry them. It was as if the adults had never been flesh and blood; that, instead, it was only the kids' ideas of them that had given them substance. As if their parents had been ghosts waiting to vanish.

Were there none who'd taken shelter elsewhere on the estate or out in the woods? As the effort wore on, the grim answer seemed to settle itself. It was midafternoon by the time they had exhumed the last of the Terrace and gathered all the dead they could find. They stood together then, facing the piled parts.

It was Rodney who posed the question of what they should do next. No one had a good answer.

Grimy and downcast, the band retreated across the court to where Dee was huddled with the youngest. Melody and Venus were hungry, she said. No one else was, but if they were going to survive, they had to consider what they might do for food. Kris suggested they look in whatever remained of her villa's kitchen.

Beth was mature for twelve, thoughtful, earnest and independent—qualities Jema had often admired. Beth was athletic too, and she defined herself by what she could do. Her brother, Brice, was thirteen and not at all like her, except for his curly red hair. He was reserved and tentative, nervous about expressing himself. When the group reached the Chancellor's villa, Kris asked Beth and Brice to lead the way, as they knew the kitchen far better than she. Their father—who'd departed with the caravan—was the villa chef.

The kitchen tiles had been fired twice—once in years past, and once the previous night. A tangle of copper pipes lay burst and melted in oily puddles. Flames had consumed the pantry and the food stored there. Dried meats and cheese, grains, breads and jams, bags of sugared fruit—all hopelessly charred. But Brice pointed at a cabinet intact at the rear, and

40

when Beth opened its scorched door, they found a half-dozen jars of gourmet treats: candied Verner's nuts, pickled fern heads, wren eggs in brine. Snugg opened the jars. Melody fished out a fern head, Venus wolfed the nuts, while the older kids watched.

"Snacks," Rangi muttered.

When Melody had swallowed the last of the fern heads, she licked her fingers and peered at Jema. "I lost my doll," she said.

Pate straightened, glancing at Rodney and Wyatt, and facing Rangi. "We need to check the meat lockers," he said. "Let's do that now."

The four boys left the others in the kitchen. They returned an hour later with a grim report. They had started at the butcher's hut, looking for the slaughtered lambs, and found them all in a blackened heap. The lockers nearby were burnt to their foundations, along with the large stores of meat inside.

The group absorbed the bad news. Then Rangi motioned to them.

He led them through the ravaged den out into the Chancellor's garden, where they seated themselves around the pool, with the scorched exotics drooping over them. The sun was sinking behind the western hills.

"We're here on this ridge," Rangi said, "with no adults and no help near. The only transportation we have is a train that goes in a circle."

"We're dead," Ry-Lynn said.

"Finished," Wyatt bowed his head.

Rangi huffed, "I'm not saying that."

Jema put her hand on Wyatt's shoulder. She'd never seen him so agitated.

"I'm still hungry," Venus whimpered to Dee, and she began to cry.

"We're not going to starve," Rangi said. "Not right away. There have to be things we can salvage, things we can use to take care of ourselves. Are you listening?"

Kris nodded.

Jema looked from face to face. "We can," she said, "I know we can." For all their differences, the kids were close. They'd been schooled together, they'd played together, they'd lived on the ridge together for many summers. The class line the grownups drew between the Governor and the gardener was, for most of the kids, a band of shadow that came and went.

"Our job right now," Rangi said, "is to find whatever we can. We'll work in three teams," he said. "You four, with me. You'll go with Kris. The rest follow Pate. We'll make a pile," he said looking over his shoulder, "by the Royal Express."

Jema turned to Melody. "Will you help?"

Melody nodded.

Rangi eyed the horizon. It was growing dark. "We'll start at dawn."

"We should do something about the grownups," Rodney reminded them.

Dee stayed in the Chancellor's garden with Melody and

Venus. The rest of the band returned to the charnel pile. As Jema approached, it seemed that color had disappeared from the world. There was only the settlement's blackened crater and a pewter sky.

When they reached the dead, Pate grabbed a board and used it to raise up earth and ash, which he scattered over the charnel. The others followed his example, doing what they could to respect their elders and to hide what couldn't be hidden.

The mound of burnt body parts, even with soil on it, was terrible to behold. When they'd done their best to cover it, the boards fell from their hands and the kids, except Rangi, knelt before it and wept. He scowled and walked back and forth like he was whetting himself for a scuffle, hips black from brushing against burnt debris. He paused beside Ry-Lynn, and Jema heard him mutter, "I didn't think Finger would do that."

Jema knelt beside a visored Wyatt. His chest heaved with sobs, hands covering his eyes. She wanted to console him, but she didn't know how. Snugg was curled a few feet from his mother.

I'll remember this, Jema thought, for the rest of my life.

When the grieving was over, the kids walked alone or with an arm around the shoulder of another, heads bowed, a defeated army in retreat. A breeze wuffed in Jema's ear, as resonant as the Governor's voice, with its cadence of empathy and care; and a moment returned—the moment in his study when, sadly and softly, he looked into her eyes and said: "I won't always be here to take care of you. Someday you'll be on your own."

They woke the next morning, formed their teams and wandered the ruins, digging and lifting, batting objects free of cinders and coals, scavenging what they could. They found food in a few dwellings—dried, cured, tinned or boxed. In a half-burnt outbuilding, they found blankets and sheets, and a bundle of towels. There were tools in the gardener's shed, and picks and shovels; from the huts they took cups and bowls, platters, spoons, forks and knives, and some cookery too— iron skillets, pots, ladles and grilling stakes, shears and spits, and a mechanical fire striker.

Pate and Rangi went to search Hunu's hut. Pate asked if Jema could come, and Rangi agreed. Their first sight of the modest dwelling damped their hopes. Little remained.

Among the ashes of his father's workbench, Rangi salvaged some saw blades and drills. Hunu's machete was good as new, and Rangi slid it through his belt. Beneath a span of charred roof, Pate found the chief's spearhead. "The old fool," Rangi muttered. "Keep it," he waved the relic away.

Jema thought of Caaqi. Had the parrot been incinerated in his cage? Had he somehow escaped the flames? She looked at Pate. He was wondering too.

The three took the path that skirted the hut. Rangi used

the machete to chop away the charred door of the shed where Hunu had kept the parrot. Jema bowed her head, fearful of what she might see. A single feather rose with the flying wood and fell to the ground by her foot, chocolate, untouched by flame. She stooped to retrieve it, and as she rose, she saw that the shed was empty, or almost empty. All that remained was the floor of the cage and the burnt stubs of the bars. No beak, no talons, no blackened body. No other trace of the bird at all.

She glanced at Pate, unsure whether to feel relief or fear. Had an earthly parrot been freed by the blaze? Or had the "author of love and bloodshed" been set loose on some frightful errand? Hunu's words seem to rise like smoke from the ashes around them.

By late afternoon, many of the huts and outbuildings had been sifted. It was then that Kris, weak and anxious, led the girls through the bedroom wing of her home. It was a maze that only she could traverse. Jema held her hand, following close.

Nothing remained of Kris' bedroom. Her parents' room, too, was mostly destroyed, but parts of her mother's wardrobe and vanity were intact. The photos, muzzed by smoke, were still on the walls—glamorous shots taken before Kris was born. Jema imagined the woman in her white robe, leaning back in the white lounge chair in a spotlight of patio glare—colorless, except for her emerald eyes and the orange

45

drink she held in her hand. She would jiggle her cubes as she spoke. Even anaesthetized, she retained her sharp opinion of others.

Her dresses hung in orderly lines, undamaged. Venus squealed to see the sequins and scales, the spangles and creped silk. The slacks were pressed; robes and shoes; and her makeup too. Kris unhooked the mirror from the wall. It was scorched around the edges, and the glass was cracked.

In a nearby vestibule, flames had consumed a collection of hats. They were shriveled and charred; and with them, a mask for a costume ball. Its painted parchment had vaporized, leaving only the wire mesh. When she raised it to her face, Kris seemed to be peering through a spider's web. She passed it to Jema. Then she ducked beneath a masonry arch and opened the liquor closet. No sign of the fire there. Kris had snuck a few samples in her mother's absence, but the closet was still well-stocked. The bottom shelves were loaded with the magazines they all prized, disclosing the torrid romances of actors and actresses.

"We'll take these, won't we?" Venus said, reaching for one.

She opened the cover and turned the pages while the girls crowded around. The celebrities were as sleek and charming as ever. Some of the paper was brittle, flaking around the edges. A wistful smile reshaped Venus' pout and her sooty cheeks.

There was a drawer of ladies' fans, hand-painted; a lace parasol; and a brass bell the woman rang at parties to signal courses or scheduled events. Dee raised it and tinkled, and the girls laughed.

"It's all ours now," Kris said. "I'm going to share it."

After the girls had hauled the booty to the scavenge pile, Jema handed off Melody to Beth and returned alone to her ruined home.

As she crossed the threshold, she remembered the day her parents departed. It would be nice, she'd thought, to be without all that badgering for a while. Her bedroom on the upper floor was gone. But her play space downstairs in the Governor's study still had its easel, and the table and chairs. They were black now, as if her old life existed in a shadow world. Using a plank to rake through the ashes, Jema found a doll from years past: a native warrior with a topknot, a hooked nose and a drum in one hand. His brown skin was worn, but his face was unburnt. When she chucked his chin, he gave a mechanical laugh, a jarring reaction to the damage nearby: all those books, all those words.

At sundown, the search was over. The kids gathered by the Royal Express. Beth and Brice selected food from the collectings, while Pate devised a functioning oven using a bucket and timber tails. Rodney had found a tarp, and he and Rangi covered the scavenged haul.

Beth and Brice's father loved his job, and they had learned a lot from him. When he left with the caravan, they'd wanted to take his place in the kitchen, but Mr. Trett wouldn't have it. Now was their chance, and they fussed between themselves about this and that while the others shared their discoveries.

"Show them the casting," Venus said.

In response, Kris lifted an object she'd taken from her mother's boudoir—a porcelain of an antique couple seated at a cafe table. The man was dressed for hunting, with a cap, vest and rifle; the woman wore a veil and raised a wine glass. Melody drew close and touched the porcelain dress.

Rangi lifted a globe of white marble, weighing it in his hand. When he tipped it up, Jema recognized the bald-headed visage of a long-dead president. For years, the bust had glared at her from the Chancellor's mantle.

"When will we leave?" Venus asked.

Rangi shook his head at the question.

"We're going back," Venus looked at Kris, "to the capital."

"How do you think we'd do that?" Kris sighed.

"There's no way to ford the rivers," Wyatt said. "We'd need rafts."

"And horses," Pate added.

Snugg looked at Jema. "They'll come back for us."

They were all thinking of the Governor and the Chancellor.

"I'm sure they will," Kris said.

Rodney put his big fingers to his lips. Venus blanched, Melody wilted; Jema knelt and pushed the warrior doll into her arms.

"We haven't done badly so far," Rangi said, facing Pate.

"We may be alright on our own," Pate agreed.

Beth continued stirring a pot, blindly. The thirteen absorbed the idea. Kris glanced at Jema with daring in her eyes.

"We need a leader," Kris said. "I nominate Rangi."

Rangi inclined his head, acting like her words made no sense to him.

"Yep," Rodney concurred.

Snugg was quick to join in, and so was Venus. Jema, realizing they'd been waiting for such a thing, added her assent. Then the rest, Pate included, affirmed the selection.

Rangi nodded slowly, pondering his assignment. It seemed to Jema that he was taking the group's confidence to heart.

When Beth and Brice had finished, they all sat on the railbed beside the loco, and the two served a stew made from food in cans and jars. They passed the steaming bowls around and the kids ate their fill, except Dee.

"You have to eat," Kris said.

"I can't," Dee replied.

Melody lowered the doll's chin, and the warrior laughed. The kids joined in.

When the meal was over, they climbed the steel grate steps of the Royal Express single file. In the humid and stuffy car, the kids reclaimed their seats and did their best to bed down, leaning together or curled tight. Jema and Pate slept with Melody across their laps.

For hours Jema felt buffets of wind. Or was the charging warmth Pate's breath in her ear? She dreamt he was near, she

49

dreamt he was far. He was moving before her through a jungle, and she was trying to catch up. He was high above her in a tree; and she was below, straining to see. He was in a world apart, the way only an orphan could be. Would she ever understand him?

She did now, in a way. Her home was gone and so were her parents.

It was the two of them, Jema and Pate, throwing in with each other. I'm lucky, she thought. I trust him. I could go on a long journey with Pate. Then she thought, We are on that journey.

At dawn the band visited the paddock. Pate had voiced his concerns about the ravaged meat lockers, and he wanted to see what remained of the flock. They found a dozen sheep and half as many lambs. The sun's rays strafed the animals' backs, and the steam rising from their woolly bodies made a golden corona, as if they were already roasting on a grill. The kids pressed their faces to the wire fence, hands clutching the welded squares.

"These won't last us long," Brice observed.

"There's meat out there," Pate said, gazing at the estate's green border.

Snugg, distraught and distracted, called for his mother. The cry carried across the pasture and into the jungle, and the contrast between the boy's yearning and the trial to come caught Jema's heart. She looked at Pate. He felt it too.

They walked through the vegetable gardens and orchards, pressing Ry-Lynn for answers. Her mother had been the arborist. "Nothing's changed for them," she said quietly. "They'll keep producing."

"There are edible things in the forest," Beth pointed out. "Bloodstalk and fawn bread. Clack nuts too."

Then Kris raised the question of shelter. "We can't stay in the train."

"I like it there," Venus said.

"You're short," Wyatt grumped. "The rest of us can't lay down."

Rodney agreed. "There's not enough room."

"We'll live in the jungle," Rangi told them.

Venus stared at him. Dee made her eyes wide but didn't speak.

After they'd put some food in their stomachs, the group considered the problem.

Below the ridge the jungle was tiered, tall roroas with mid-story trees layered beneath, and a cover of shrubs and ferns crowding the earth. Only the train tracks breached the native side, but on the capital side a path led through the forest, and there were places the kids had played. With Rangi in the lead, they descended to have a look.

The stands were dense and shady, the majestic roroa rising around them, massive in girth and perfectly straight. The trunks were rugged, with platy bark stained by lichen and shelved with fungus ears that often circled a tree to its top. Branchless for most of their height, in the upper reaches the roroa released emerald clouds, millions of tear-shaped leaves. The understory was crowded with saplings and sinuous vines all woven together, a myriad windows of green glass leaded with branches black and gray and the color of brick. As the kids reached the end of the path, a flock of birds rose from the weft, hovering above them. Rangi halted, the others gathered around and the birds descended, disappearing back into the bush.

"Somewhere in there," Rangi pointed.

The kids looked at the green tangle, trying to imagine.

They continued forward, winding between the giant trunks, through fern beds and bogs, pushing vines and creepers aside. Jema was frightened at first. The forest is swallowing us, she thought. Melody gripped her hand, snuffling while the breeze *whished* through the branches. Jema looked back, glanced at Pate, then faced forward again.

After a stretch of what seemed aimless wandering, Rangi halted, turning, looking around. "Not a bad spot."

"It's flat," Kris said.

Pate nodded. "We'd be out of the wind."

"We'll cut down some trees," Rangi proposed, "and make a roof to put over our heads." He spread his hands, palms up, imagining rain.

"No walls?" Dee asked.

"We have to get tougher," Rangi said.

Kris shook her head. "We're not going to live like savages."

Rangi bristled.

"Does anyone know how to build a house?" Wyatt said.

There was silence. Melody burrowed into Jema's thigh, whimpering. Jema could feel the tremor in her hip and the bones of her leg.

"I have an idea," Ry-Lynn muttered. There was something about the others' dread that seemed to shake her out of her own. Her mother had been proficient on the loom, she reminded them. Ry-Lynn knew a fair bit about weaving. Her idea was to make shelters out of branches and vines.

"We could cut off branches," she explained, "bury the ends in the ground and tie them together at the top. Then we'd weave vines through them." They could use Verner's Coil, she said, pointing at a skein nearby. "It's strong and it grows really fast." The leaves were tough and it produced no fruit, so the shelters wouldn't be pecked by birds. And the pink flowers would brighten the shelters in the spring, assuming they were still alive.

Ry-Lynn looked at Kris.

"I like it," Kris said.

Pate thought the idea might work. "If we padded the insides with moss," he said, "it would keep the warmth in."

How long could they live in the shelters? Jema wondered. How much time would pass before her parents returned?

Rangi was silent. He seemed glad for Ry-Lynn's solution

but was annoyed, Jema saw, that the idea had come from someone else. He reasserted his command by assigning tasks.

Rodney and Wyatt returned to the salvage pile, and once they had tools, the kids began. The boys cut down branches and the girls stripped off the leaves, and together they secured the butt ends in the soil and tipped them together. Pate cinctured the joining with a length of vine. Working on the shelters helped to diffuse their fear and blunt their grief.

In two days they erected frames for three shelters in a line, then they added a fourth and fifth on either side. It was a peaceful spot, Jema thought. And there was a window of sky downhill.

On the third day, they began stringing Verner's Coil, planting the root end of each in the ground and weaving them through the frames, leaving an opening to come and go. Weaving the vines was a painstaking task. The old Ry-Lynn was back—she bossed the job harshly, impatient and particular, carping nonstop. But the result was a good one: the windings were tight and flawless. Despite her insults and Rangi's bluster, a feeling of kinship fell over them all. Beneath the roroas' filtering crowns, the light on their faces looked different—softer, gentler. They might have been cherubs in an antique painting. Melody was, for the first time, not clutching anyone's hand.

It took two days to gather moss and dry grass to line the walls and floors. Completed, each shelter looked like a dust devil with a minaret top, an apt impression given the speed with which they'd been assembled.

Rangi staked out bathrooms nearby, pits covered with fern fronds. He announced that a rill downslope would be their water source, and he made Rodney "Hauler." At the end of each day, Rodney would refill a barrel with pails they'd found in the gardener's shed. After that, Rangi told each of them where they would sleep. "These shelters are for the girls," he said. "Jema and Melody will be here at the rear. Kris will be by the opening."

Once he'd made the assignments, the kids started back to the Royal Express to gather up their things. Jema walked with Kris. Her best friend was near tears.

"He couldn't have put me farther away from him," Kris said.

"It's not you," Jema replied. "He's separated Pate and me too."

"He didn't have to do that," Kris said.

"No, he didn't," Jema agreed.

But they'd chosen him as their chief. What complaint could they make? Kris squinted, watching Rangi leading the gang up the trail.

Before they bedded down that night, the leader addressed the group.

"We have to take care of ourselves," Rangi said, "and there aren't any grownups to tell us how. We'll need rules to live together," he said, "and we'll have to obey them. Everything will be shared." He looked at Kris. "We're all equal now."

Dee raised her hand. "I have to go. Can I use the bathroom?"

Beth waved. "I have to go too." She followed Dee.

Venus shouted, "I'm coming," and headed after them.

Rodney and Snugg were assigned to a shelter with Pate. Rangi had Wyatt and Brice with him. Jema coaxed Melody through the entrance of their shelter. Then she stood there alone, watching darkness settle over the jungle, imagining her father in another world wishing the best for her.

The establishment of the forest camp went smoothly. Pate turned a straight branch into a shaft for his cannibal spearhead and used the weapon to slaughter two of the lambs in the paddock. They set a small amount aside for the evening meal, divided the rest into rations, wrapped them carefully, and stored them in a crate below ground. Then they talked about what they might find in the wild. The chefs had depended on fish and elk, and Rodney's dad had led trips to lower elevations to hunt and net them. In the jungle, there were eels. They lived in the streams, and traveled through the woods in wriggling droves. "Ick," Venus said. "Count me out," Wyatt agreed. Jema remembered the time Hunu caught one. Glossy and black, and thick as a man's leg, eels had been part of the native diet in ages past.

Pate and Wyatt felled trees and Brice collected boughs, stocking a woodpile for the oven and a friendly fire around which they gathered at night. Beth and her brother cut

Whistling Reeds that grew along the edges of a nearby stream. Their father had used the reeds as skewers for grilling.

Ry-Lynn oversaw the gardens and orchards, and Snugg and Rodney helped with the harvests. Rangi knew how to drive the Royal Express, so they used the train to move fruits and vegetables to the head of the footpath leading into the forest. Ry-Lynn led forays into the jungle as well, where Jema and Melody helped her collect fawn bread and roroa jam. The bread was a fungus that rose from tree bark in spongy sheets when it rained. In places, it shrouded trunks and branches. Roroa jam was sap that dripped from the trees' trunks. It was sweet and tasted of vanilla and almond. A treat could be made with fawn bread and the jam spread on top, a remembered comfort they all enjoyed, even Dee. It rained every day in the midafternoon, a chilly event now that fall had descended. But not so chilly that, when they were dirty, they couldn't stand in the downpour to clean themselves and use salvaged towels to dry off. At night Melody took care of her warrior doll, feeding and comforting him. They knew she'd fallen asleep when the doll's mechanical laughter stopped.

Despite their new home's many blessings, the question of meat cast an ugly shadow. "The poor things," Dee lamented. She'd developed an affection for the sheep. Everyone else thought the grilled meat was tasty, but they were going through it quickly.

Three weeks after the erection of the shelters, Pate slaughtered what remained of the flock. And three weeks after that,

Beth told the group over dinner, "That's the last of the ribs and muscle. It's fatty stew from here on. And there's not very much."

"Elk. Boar and wallaby," Rangi nodded, pointing through the trees. "It's a grocery out there. Rodney and I are going shopping tomorrow."

Brice gave a rousing shout.

"Does he know what he's doing?" Jema said.

"We'll find out," Pate replied.

The next evening, Rangi and Rodney returned empty-handed. The latter sat silent while Rangi recounted exciting chases, near catches and unlikely escapes. The stories sounded like nonsense to Jema. Pate shook his head and laughed.

Aside from fears of starvation, Jema saw, most were struggling with their new existence. Putting the grownups out of their heads was hard for Snugg and Wyatt. Venus seemed to imagine the fire was a punishment she'd earned for bad behavior. Kris had mixed feelings about her parents. She missed them, she said, but she couldn't help feeling that they'd abandoned her. Jema thought about the violence in the capital. Had the insurrection been quelled? Maybe her mother and father were on their way back.

Rangi fought his doubt with defiance. "It's chance," he told them one night around the fire. "And a good chance, at that. You'll all feel better when there's plenty of meat." He kicked off his shoes. "They're falling apart," he complained. "I can't hunt in those things."

"I could try to repair them," Ry-Lynn offered.

Jema looked at Pate. "I don't think the problem with the hunt is his shoes."

Two days later, after eating the last of the sheep for dinner, Rangi called for a celebration. They had their own tribe now, he said. "We're surviving without the grownups. Working together, respecting each other."

Jema was stunned. He wanted admiration. He wanted to be recognized as a leader. But he didn't understand the responsibilities. Or he didn't care. She was seated beside Kris, and Kris was watching him too, but she seemed unbothered.

Rangi spread his arms. "I say: let's loosen up. Kris found poison in her mom's closet. What do you think?"

Wyatt whooped, taking the cue.

"I'm for that." Kris lifted her chin. "Let's get bashed."

"Without food," Jema muttered, "we won't survive."

"Stop worrying," Kris told her.

Jema turned to Pate, who was standing behind her. He inclined his head as if hearing a familiar sound. "We're all feeling danger," he said.

The bottles appeared and liquor was poured into cups. When Jema heard the twist of the caps and the unchaste gurgles, she remembered Kris' mom. The odor of liquor mixed with the woman's perfume was a combination as pungent as manure. A few kids sampled the stuff and found the taste harsh. But they did their best to down the drinks with showy zeal.

"I think," Kris waved her glass at the group, "we need some new rags." And she directed Dee and Ry-Lynn to haul out the trunk in which she'd stored her mother's clothing.

Kris selected a fur stole for Beth and a wrap for Dee. As the two put the attire on over their grimy clothes, Kris had Ry-Lynn set up the scorched mirror and the girls took turns posing, arranging and rearranging, admiring their reflections. The glass had spoking cracks, and the pieces were loose, so as they mugged and strutted before it, parts of their bodies came and went.

Rangi dashed more liquor into his cup, raised the bottle to Beth and strode toward her. She accepted a cup, took a swallow and began to cough. Wyatt laughed.

For Jema, Kris picked out a white blouse with ruffles and a black shawl.

Jema stepped forward reluctantly and tried them on. Maybe Kris was right, she thought. Nice clothing always lifted your spirits.

For Ry-Lynn, Kris selected what looked like a naval officer's jacket with brass tassels and epaulettes. For Venus a cape, and a striped scarf for Melody. For herself Kris chose a long purple gown, sequined and shimmering.

Venus looked at herself in the mirror, lifting the wings of her cape and eyeing Kris in the fractured reflection. "What was it like being the Chancellor's daughter?" she mused out loud.

Rangi was entertained, and so were the other boys, Pate included. The costumery seemed to draw them together. Rangi faced Jema and approached her with an empty cup.

She watched him fill the cup to the brim, and she accepted it from him without objecting. They were carrying a heavy
burden. Perhaps it would be a good thing to lighten it.

"The boys too," Kris shouted. She retrieved a fleece vest
and handed it to Rodney.

He put it on, but it was so small he couldn't move his
arms.

Dee hooted and pointed, and Venus joined in. Kris handed a floppy hat to Snugg.

Jema took a sip—she didn't like it—then another sip—
she didn't like that either. Then she closed her eyes and
downed the whole glass.

Rodney looked ridiculous—a trained bear in a wool
vest—with Snugg prancing beside him like a dwarfish clown.

"And for our leader," Kris shouted, "something special."
She pulled a pair of white silk pajamas from the trunk, along
with a golden scarf. Kris held out the garments to Rangi, who
surprised everyone by roaring his approval and hurrying to
accept them.

Jema saw Pate by the fire, wearing the black wire mask.
As she watched, he tipped a bottle, filling his cup. She hurried
toward him, spreading her shawl as she closed the distance,
encircling Pate's head in a dark cocoon and kissing his lips.

A cheer sounded. Did Pate like this, she thought, as much
as she did? Over his shoulder Jema saw: she wasn't the only one
giving way to her impulses. Ry-Lynn whispered in Wyatt's ear,
squeezing his shoulder. Snugg's eyes were glued on Beth. Venus,
knowing Rangi was watching, twirled before the mirror, mak-

ing eyes and mouths; and then Rangi stepped closer and faced the glass, beholding himself in his white pajamas.

Venus applauded. Others joined in.

Rangi motioned Kris toward him so the shattered reflection could capture them both. "My purple queen," he said. She beamed and bumped her hip against his.

Even Melody, it seemed, felt seduction in the air. She'd found a tube of lipstick in the trunk and was painting her lips with it.

They looked like a theater troupe, jabbering and skipping around the fire. Rangi sauntered among them like a sultan with Kris on his arm, the happiest Jema had ever seen her.

Rangi halted and raised his face to the jungle canopy. Then, in a public way, he removed his pajama top and stripped off his shirt.

What is he doing? Jema thought. She marked again his muscled shoulders, the chest of a man—broad, native and coppered. The others were seeing it too.

"A physical test," he announced, lowering his gaze to scan the group. "And a test of daring too." He pointed at a nearby roroa. "We're going to climb that tree, using its ears."

Kris stared at him. Dee looked confused.

Was he serious? Jema wondered.

The semicircular fungi at the base of a tree were often as wide as a man was high. As the trunk tapered, the ears grew smaller, sprouting at regular intervals around it like a spiral staircase. Rangi pulled off his pants and undergarments.

The band was struck silent. "Look at that," Kris said.

Perfectly naked, Rangi strode toward the trunk. Melody hid her face, Venus was plum-eyed. Then Rodney laughed and stripped off his clothes, and Brice did the same. It wasn't lust, Jema realized. The nudity expressed a spirit of freedom and the flouting of rules.

Pate stepped forward, removing his shirt. Jema followed him.

Rangi cried out, boosted himself onto the first ear and swung to the second, using a long stride, gripping the bark with both hands. Kris was hurrying toward the base of the tree, still in her regal purple. Rodney, Wyatt and Brice, all naked, were right behind her.

Had Rangi done this before? A thrilling feat, but a dangerous one. The steps weren't all firmly attached. Fallen ears were littered around the feet of old trees. He moved to the next ear and the next—up and around the massive trunk, leaping from ear to ear. Then a second cry sounded. More than a cry of triumph: it was a summons.

Kris was at the foot of the lofty roroa now. Rodney, Wyatt and Brice were approaching, and so was Pate. Jema hurried after them. As she moved, the sun's fanning radials shifted, and where the raying gold passed through a gap in the aerial vault, she saw a creature perched on a branch. A large bird in silhouette.

Caaqi is here, Jema thought. Or was he? There were many parrots in the jungle. Still, the silhouette seemed like an omen. If this was Caaqi, why had he come? Had he been watching them?

Kris threw herself at the giant trunk, leaping, ascending its ears, repeating Rangi's moves. And boys followed behind her—Rodney, then Wyatt, Brice and Pate.

Something terrible is going to happen, Jema thought. She halted, open-mouthed, heart missing its beat.

Rangi was halfway up now. Ry-Lynn was cheering him on. Venus clapped, frightened for him but greatly impressed. The others followed, with Pate at the rear. Come down, Jema thought. Come down, come down—

As the ears grew smaller, Rangi's pace quickened. He circled the trunk again and again, approaching the top. Cold drops were falling on Jema's face. Melody was at her knee, hanging on. She lifted the child in her arms, feeling the wind rising.

Rangi reached the top and circled his arm, rounding up the storm. Kris rose just below him, clasping his waist, looking up. What did she want of him? Recognition, Jema thought. And then, to the surprise of all who watched, Rangi put his arms around her, drew her up and put his lips to hers, wobbling drunkenly all the while, risking a plunge at any moment. The kids were shouting and laughing, and then the storm burst and rain poured down.

Rangi was descending, and so was Kris, gown soaked, hair lashing. They passed Rodney, who was zippering up with Wyatt and Brice behind him. Pate was last. All were naked and glistening, climbing quickly.

"Is Pate safe?" Melody asked.

Jema was mute, watching his every move. He was approaching the tree's top.

Rangi reached the ground and raised both arms, striding forward, victorious. Venus cried out and sent him a swooning look. Kris followed behind him, dragging her drenched gown.

Wyatt and Brice were descending now, and so was Rodney. As Pate reached the roroa's top, one of the ears broke loose and he lost his footing. He hung for a moment, legs dangling as the rotten fungus fell to the forest floor. Jema cried out, Melody raised her hand, trying to help. Together they watched Pate wrap his arms around the trunk and slide till he reached the next ear. At the same time, the sky grew darker. Then a flood was released, and water came down in a heedless torrent.

Pate disappeared. "Where is he?" Melody fretted. Jema didn't reply.

And then the rainy curtain drew back, and they saw him descending. The ears' upper sides were concave, and they trapped water. Jema could see a splash with each step he took. The ears were overflowing, turning the tree into a spiral fountain.

Lightning flashed over the sealed canopy. Pate was descending through the downpour like a hero in fable, while the thunder sounded and the wind shook the branches. Wyatt, Rodney and Brice had reached the bottom and were leaping after Rangi.

It seemed impossible Pate would make it down, but he did. As he reached the earth, a cheer went up. And then he was reeling, laughing and stumbling toward her. Jema received his embrace, with Melody pressed between them. She kissed his brow, his cheek, his lips, and all around them the wind howled and rain fell in cracking sheets.

High in the jungle's crown, backlit by a luminous web, Jema saw the great parrot spread his wings and go sailing through the storm, as if his mission—whatever it was—had been fulfilled.

The next morning, the sun found its way back to them. The ears on the trees had pools clear and fresh, so the kids removed their clothes and climbed up to bathe in one or another. The boys were at the far end of the grove, the girls by the shelters.

Jungle birds, brightly colored, came to bathe with them, alighting on the rims of ears, hovering among them, diving and bobbing, threshing crystal beads from their wings. The kids were sober now, and none the worse for their spree—but rather nerved and encouraged by it. The sun shone on clean faces, on warmed backs and limbs, and their expressions of cheer and satisfaction filtered through the camp and into the jungle.

That afternoon Pate and Jema went for a walk. They were

both barefoot. Pate had a red scrape on his shin from the broken ear. Jema's hair was clean but tangled. She'd bound it up with a short length of vine. With Kris' permission, she took the lace parasol with her.

"It was a relief," Jema confessed, "to forget about whether we're going to starve."

"Rangi eased the pressure," Pate said. "But we have to do something. Soon."

She felt like a foolish child, with her dreams of romance, and the suspicions, bred by Hunu, that some mysterious power was circling around them.

"When you were climbing the tree last night," Jema said, "I thought I saw Caaqi nearby. On a limb. Watching." She looked in Pate's eyes. "It frightened me."

Pate said nothing.

"And—" Jema pursed her lips.

"And?" he prompted her.

"I thought I saw him the night the villas burned down, flying over the fire." Jema sighed. "Strange ideas."

They stepped into a clearing where the sun shone through.

"Is he threatening us?" Jema said. "Protecting us? Is he watching us, even now?"

She let the parasol sag onto her shoulder and scanned the treetops.

The jungle was just a jungle. There was no sign of Caaqi.

Pate's blue eyes fixed on her. "You're beautiful," he said.

She smiled and laughed, rotating the parasol.

Then she stopped, faced him and used her free hand to remove a leaf stuck to his ear. She had always hoped the two would fall in love.

Pate drew close, and his kiss had a warmth and depth she'd never felt before.

3

Tema stepped through a break in the foliage and Pate followed. The camp's shelters came into view, and then the smoking firepit with the kids squatting around it.

Another six weeks had passed. Repeated attempts had been made to find game, without success. And maintaining the gardens and orchards proved harder than they had imagined. The beds needed fertilizer, Ry-Lynn recalled after a wave of wilting; then a blight struck the trees. It was winter now, not as cold as in the capital, but chilly still, especially at night. Many of the wild foods in the forest had vanished. The band was hungry and weak. There was only so much fawn bread and jam they could eat.

There was talk of leaving. With the cold, Wyatt pointed out, the rivers would shrink. They might not need rafts to ford them. Rangi gave Rodney his machete and sent him down the trail toward the capital. Rodney returned two days later, torn up by thorns. He hadn't reached water. The track was grown over. "It's impassable," he said.

The sun had descended, and the tribe was hugging the fire.

As Jema approached, she saw Rangi on the far side of the pit, flanked by Kris. Kris used every pretext to be close to him, but she wasn't getting the attention she craved. Alone in their shelter at night, Jema tried to cheer her up. But the attempts seemed only to hurt their friendship. Perhaps the hunger and cold was straining that too.

"Where were you?" Rangi demanded of her and Pate.

Pate, now accustomed to the leader's bile, ignored him.

Rangi motioned for them to sit, then he scanned the faces and drew a breath, steeling himself.

"I'm making new rules," he said, "and we're all going to follow them. The boys' only job is to hunt and bring back meat." He waited for the boys to nod. "The girls will take charge of everything else. They'll harvest what they can from the farm and fields. They'll do the cooking and take care of our shelters." He paused.

Jema waited for her friend to object, but Kris was nodding. Before the villas' destruction, Jema thought, Rangi's volatile temper and his appetite for rebellion made him the first to be punished and the last to obey. Things were different now.

"If a boy kills an animal," Rangi said, "one we can eat, he'll be honored by all, myself included. He will eat first, before the rest of us. The girls will serve him."

Again Jema looked at Kris, expecting some resistance.

"That's right," she said. "Whoever brings meat, we'll serve him."

Wyatt drew his visor down. Snugg elbowed Rodney. The boys had spent the past week fashioning weapons, binding blades onto hafts and poles to make knives and spears. Brice had whittled a club from a fallen bough. Beth had sewn together bedrolls and tarps for the hunters, using sheets and blankets they'd salvaged.

"We're leaving together," Rangi said, "and we're not coming back empty-handed."

"You're in charge while I'm gone," Rangi told Kris.

"We'll light a big fire," she said, "when you return." Kris faced the girls. "We'll start gathering the wood right now."

A nice gesture by Rangi, Jema thought. It was good to see Kris exercising her authority, even if it was to serve Rangi's requests. Kris assigned tasks to each of them, and the girls set to work, clearing ash from the pit, gathering kindling, grabbing fallen branches and dragging them closer.

The boys left a few minutes later. Jema and the others paused in their work and watched as the hunters ascended a slope single file, turned along a streambed and vanished into the jungle.

Just before Rangi disappeared, Venus waved at him and blew him a kiss.

"What do you think you're doing?" Kris demanded.

"He can't keep his eyes off me," Venus replied.

Kris' face froze. "You're pathetic," she said.

Venus was mute. Her lips were trembling.

"You've frightened her," Jema told her best friend.

"Good," Kris said, staring back, anger roiling in her green eyes.

Four days later, the boys returned. Beth saw them approaching, and a shout went up. Kris retrieved the fire striker and summoned the girls to the pit.

None of the boys spoke. They trudged into camp with their heads down, except for Pate, who eyed Jema with tenderness, happy to see her. Rodney's shirt was muddy, Wyatt's pants were torn at the knees. What had they caught, Jema wondered. Were their packs laden with meat?

Kris motioned and the girls followed behind her.

She hailed Rangi. "Success?" she asked.

He didn't reply. He strode past her without a word. None of the other boys volunteered anything, but Jema could tell from Pate's stoic look that things hadn't gone well.

"Wyatt saw a warty boar," Rangi said. "Brice clubbed a bullfrog."

He jabbed his machete into the ground outside his shelter, while the others removed packs and set down their weapons. One by one, they disappeared into the huts.

Kris seemed to forget herself. Her shoulders sagged and the toughness leached from her face. She approached Rangi's shelter, dropping to her knees by the entrance. She was silent for a long moment, then she began to speak.

"We're all worried," Kris said. "We're all afraid of what might happen to us."

She was trying to comfort him, and when he didn't respond, she tried harder.

"You're our strength," she said, mixing her own insecurity with the welfare of the camp. "You're the one we need."

The girl who so often harangued others for being weak was mawkishly so, and when Jema looked around her, she could see that Kris' weakness was shaking the girls.

Rangi barked an order at her. It was liquor he wanted.

Without rising, Kris nodded to Ry-Lynn, who hurried to the trunk to retrieve a bottle.

Jema glanced at Beth, and the two motioned the others away. Jema picked up Melody, who was oblivious, tending her doll, smoothing his topknot.

An hour later, their leader emerged from his shelter.

The girls, with Jema's guidance, had lit the wood in the firepit. Pate, after washing his face and hands, had joined them, and so had Rodney and Snugg. The sky was gray, and they were gathered around the flames, huddled in blankets.

Rangi tramped to the pit with the empty bottle in his hand, glaring, indignant. He hurled the bottle, and it shattered on a rock. Kris stepped beside him.

"Get away from me," he snarled.

A spiteful sound emerged from Kris' lips. Wyatt stood and so did Pate.

"What good are you?" Rangi looked from Kris to Jema, including Dee and Venus in a sneer of dismissal. "More mouths to feed."

Kris threw herself at him in what Jema thought might be the start of a forced embrace. Then Kris' arm came around, slapping his face.

Rangi shook off the blow with a derisive laugh. "They could strip for us," he grumbled.

To the surprise of all, Snugg laughed back.

Dee's jaw dropped.

"What do you say?" Rangi challenged Rodney.

Seeing it was expected of him, Rodney laughed, and then Wyatt and Brice.

Pate edged beside Jema and took her hand.

"You're a beast," Kris told Rangi, flush with contempt.

Rangi's eyes sparkled like broken glass. He laughed again, but this laugh was strained. His gaze darted among them, as if they were all his accusers. There was no sound now but the fire crackling. Jema looked at Pate. Melody was no longer tending her doll. She understood what was happening.

Rangi lifted his chin. He raised his hand and combed his fingers through his hair, reassuming the mantle of leadership.

"I've been easy on you," he said. The words left his lips slowly, his eyes narrowing like some malign presence was ripening inside him. "What happens if we're starving? There have to be rules."

Silence.

"If someone is going to die," Rangi said, "they must be eaten before the meat spoils."

Venus gasped.

"Get out," Ry-Lynn said.

"It's you we should eat," Kris told him. "Go back to the jungle. Cannibal." She spoke now as the Chancellor's daughter. Jema could hear that, and so could the others.

"I'm in charge," Rangi said, "and according to me—" He stopped, seeing the reaction to his tyrant words. "This is a democracy," he allowed. "We all have a say." He looked at the boys. "Am I right?"

The boys nodded as one.

"All in favor of eating the weak before they spoil," Rangi said.

The boys raised their hands. Then, as one, they burst out laughing.

Beth looked at Brice, disbelieving. Melody began to cry.

"We're not voting," Kris spoke for the girls.

Rangi stared at her. "You're soft," he said, "but you'll be tasty."

The boys found that funny.

Jema caught Pate laughing with the rest. When their eyes met, the laughter froze in his throat.

Rangi seemed to relent. "I'm fooling with you," he told

Kris. "Everyone's scared. I'm just trying to lighten things up. Come on. We'll all go for a ride on the Royal Express."

"Count me out," Kris said.

"Don't be like that."

"I have no interest in your amusements," Kris said.

Rangi turned to Jema. "What about you?"

"We'll come," Pate answered for both of them.

At his words, Kris faced them with a blazing look.

Pate bowed his head, as if to ward off her wrath. "The Express may remind us of happier times."

Jema was speechless. She had never seen hatred for her in Kris' eyes. What had for so long been a vital sympathy and kinship seemed to have vanished.

The red loco was waiting, patient as a horse. Behind the depot was a shed full of wood cut to size and stacked. At Rangi's direction, they loaded the fuel box and kindled the fire, and with a belch of gray smoke the loco puffed to life. Dee didn't think her stomach could stand the ride, so Jema left Melody in her care. With Pate and the others, Jema climbed into the passenger car. Rangi yanked the steam whistle, and when he opened the throttle, the Royal Express shuddered and began to move.

They left the depot on a curving descent, picking up speed quickly. Jema opened her window and put her head out, seeing the tracks raying ahead, bright as mercury. She'd never driven the train, but when she rode in the cab with her father, she saw what he did. The controls were simple—there was a throttle and a brake. The throttle was a stick that rose from the floor, the brake was a grip that stuck out of the dash. Between the Governor's feet, there was a silver cylinder loaded with sand. When rain slicked the tracks, he released the sand to make the wheels grab.

The kids opened the windows, and as the train raced down the slope, sun lit the boys' faces and the wind blew back the girls' hair. Jema felt the joy and camaraderie that had so often prevailed on the Governor's rides. As the wheels passed over the rail gaps, a *clack-clack* sounded, recalling the Solstice Party with napkins flying and teacups rattling.

But this was no party, and the Governor wasn't in control. Rangi was driving, and through the car's forward window, Jema could see him tippling from a fresh bottle. The train was speeding toward the foot of the viaduct bridge, where the suspended tracks crossed a deep canyon; and then they were shooting across it, seeing the jungle on either side. With exhaust trailing back, the loco trundled around a cutting, skirted an abutment and zagged up a hillside. Then the track's radius shrank and the grade fell.

The peaked mouth of a tunnel appeared ahead. The Governor called it "The Soprano's Gullet," but as the loco drew closer, the entrance looked more like Caaqi's throat. The shells of his beak were open, and they were plunging into a black screaming of wheels and rails.

Jema held her breath and reached for Pate's hand. Was

he as fearful as she was? Did he feel this sense of fault and wrongdoing, that they'd made some grievous misstep, committed some crime and were all just waiting for the sentence to be pronounced?

When they returned to camp, Rangi sank to his knees and retched into the fire. The other kids watched in silence. He rose and wobbled to his hut, and for a moment, Jema felt sorry for him.

That night, the group went without dinner. Jema took Melody's hand and led her to their shelter, and Pate went with them. As they passed a roroa, Jema saw Kris leaning against the trunk with her arms folded across her chest. Jema slowed, seeing the embers of her friend's eyes through the shadows.

"Enjoy the ride?" Kris spoke in a low voice.

"I'm sorry we went," Jema said.

She waited for Kris to reply, but there was only silence.

Pate urged Jema forward. When they reached the shelter, he stooped to embrace Melody. Then he rose and kissed Jema goodnight, telling her that he was going to wake early the next morning and leave the camp without saying goodbye.

"The hunting party," he said, "took orders from Rangi. I have a different idea."

Two days later, just before dark, Jema was with Beth preparing fawn bread. The kids were despondent and listless, hashing over how much longer they could survive on their dwindling stores and what they were gleaning from the forest and gardens. Jema had told them why Pate had vanished, and there were speculations about where he'd gone and what he intended. But no one, including Jema, knew.

It was Beth who spotted him approaching the camp, on the track that descended from the ridge's spine. When Jema looked up, he was carrying his spear in one hand and supporting a log on his back, draped across his shoulders like an oxen yoke. Hanging from the log were four limp eels, each staring skyward, black-skinned and shiny, their bodies so long the tails dragged on the ground. The eels' heads were triangular and they joggled, mouths gaping, teeth bared.

Jema shouted and ran to meet him, adding her strength to his, lifting the weight from his shoulders. He winced as the burden left him. Beth was hurrying toward them, and Ry-Lynn as well.

"Your back must be raw," Jema said.

Together the girls lifted the log, and with Pate's help they carried it into the camp, bounty swinging, the eels' eyes rimmed with gold. Jema touched one. The black skin was slimy.

Rodney and Snugg came running. Kris hurried forward, with Venus behind her, eyeing the frightful catch. In moments, they were gathered around.

"Where did you find them?" Rodney asked Pate.

Venus tapped an eel's head with her finger as if to wake it.

Jema could see Rangi between two shelters, his face turned their way, watching. He took a few strides toward them, then halted. Jema clasped Pate's arm, but the next moment Rangi turned and headed into the forest.

Beth urged the group toward an altar of planks that she and her brother used to prepare food. There, the eels were unbound from the log and stretched out.

Snugg frowned at the creatures, uncertain if they could really be eaten. He'd been gnawing on bitter lettuce and bloodstalk, a wild herb that natives had used to paint their faces, and his fingers and teeth were stained red.

Beth pulled a large butcher knife from a bucket and approached the altar holding it point up. "How should I do this?"

Pate regarded her. "Take out the parts you don't think we should eat."

She nodded, set the blade behind the head of the largest eel and pressed down. The blade didn't break the skin. She leaned forward, put her full weight on it and the blade sank. The severed head fell to one side, and the body of the eel began a slow writhe.

Ry-Lynn shrieked, Venus jumped back. Snugg moved closer to the eel's head, looking into its glassy eye. Beth gripped its body and used her knife to split it in half. Jema drew beside Pate, circling his waist with her arm, unconcerned about what the others might see or think.

Dee was hurrying forward with Melody. Wyatt and Brice came too.

Kris faced Pate with a grudging look. "The girls will serve you," she said.

"I don't want that."

"It's what we agreed to," Kris said.

Pate looked at Jema. "What do you think?"

Jema answered Kris. "I think we should eat together."

Kris sneered, and once again Jema saw the roots of hatred. There was a barrier between them now, and it transformed whatever Jema might say or do into something Kris found demeaning, something that further threatened their friendship.

The moon had risen above the treetops when they sampled the eels. They were gathered around the fire, pulling pieces of greasy meat off the skewers and putting them between their lips. The taste was new for all, as eel wasn't eaten in the villas or in the cottages either. Jema chewed slowly.

"How did you catch them?" Snugg asked.

Pate swallowed. "With a length of vine bound to the end of a branch. I used a green thorn for a hook. Stuck a big cricket on it."

Skewers were roasting over the coals, and the Whistling Reeds shrilled while the meat squirmed and spit.

"The hardest part," Pate said, "was pulling them out. They're heavy. They're strong and they fight. Those teeth are as sharp as carpenters' nails. As soon as I got one onto the bank, I stabbed its head with my spear."

Ry-Lynn looked at her skewer and cleared her throat.

Venus pointed. "It's Rangi," she said.

They turned to see their leader stepping toward them. Jema glanced at Pate. The kids rose to their feet.

Rangi surveyed the group, sniffing the smoky air.

"Good work," he nodded to Pate. "At least we won't starve." The recognition came with a proudful smirk, implying that Pate was attracted to lowly tasks and suited for them.

"Eels will do," Rangi said, "until we find better."

It had rained the night before. Heads of wheel moss had soaked up the water, and the climbers binding trunks and branches looked like wet rope. The roroa roots, shiny and cinnamon red, twisted through the sodden mulch.

Jema and Pate, following the tracks of the Royal Express, had reached the start of the viaduct bridge. A cool mist rose from below. The drop seemed immense. The rails were slick, the crossties slippery. Pate reached in his coat pocket, pulled out a piece of dried eel and handed it to her. She took a bite and handed it back.

"Careful," he said, eyeing the earth beneath their feet as if saying goodbye to it. Then he started across the bridge, walking between the rails. Jema followed, taking quick steps without looking down.

"He's a child," Pate said.

His harshness surprised her. But Pate was right, she thought. If they were going to survive, they had to grow up.

"We have to be more like you," she said. Pate was shorter than Rangi and not outspoken the way a leader must be. But he was more of a man.

For two weeks, Pate had hunted eels for the group. With

plentiful meat and the girls attending to things in camp, Rangi and the boys had devoted themselves to hauling wood and riding the train. The girls could hear the rumble and puff, and the piping whistle; they would catch a glimpse of the loco through a gap in the foliage and see the boys sparring on a flat car as the train wound its way through the trees.

She paid them little mind. Her heart was full of Pate, and her head was crowded with thoughts, daring and urgent—thoughts that came with an exhilaration like the one she felt now, midway across the viaduct bridge, suspended in space. The dark wall of the canyon appeared. Ferns battened the rock with green ladders all the way to the bottom.

The jungle and its wildness seemed irreparably far from the Governor's villa and her younger self. And the capital seemed even farther than that. What had happened to her parents, she wondered. Were they even alive? How long would she remain in this untamed place? What was possible here? What did she want? Who was she really?

Whatever her new life might bring, she wanted Pate to be close to her.

When they reached the far side, he stopped and turned. He saw the look in her eyes, and because he was Pate, he could sense her thoughtfulness and her deep regard. He drew closer and put his lips to hers. In the private warmth, their tongues touched. Pate pressed his hips against hers. She could feel the hardness between his thighs.

"Look," Pate said.

He turned and pointed, and Jema saw it.

Beyond the bridge moorings was a roroa grove, and at its center was a lit clearing. And on the border of the clearing was a hollow with an arbor of Caaqi's Breath. Its magenta trumpets were unmistakable.

"It's time, Jema." Pate spoke softly. "This is the place."

"You've been here before?" she asked.

Pate shook his head.

The place, she thought. "For us," she murmured.

And she gave him her hand.

He took it without a word and led her toward the arbor.

The quiet was broken only by the snap of twigs and the crush of leaf litter beneath their feet. She was nervous, yes. But confident too. The grove seemed woven with magic.

It was like a Great Room erected in a time primeval, before there were people. A hushed place where sunlight slanting through the green vaults set insect swarms whirling. Great pillars towered on either side, and before them, the bower of Caaqi's Breath was like the entrance to a cave: a comber of green loomed above, with dozens of trumpet blooms hanging down.

Magenta, the color Jema loved as a child. She would rise early to see the sky full of it when the sun was still hidden beneath the horizon. As she grew older, the color retreated to the back of her mind. But the memory was there and so was the fascination.

The soil of the grove was soft with moss and the flesh of rotting giants.

They halted at the threshold of the trumpet bower. The flaring mouths glowed where the sun edged them. The protruding anthers were powdered with gold.

The sight of that powder— For a moment, Jema imagined Caaqi emerging from a cloud of it, while the glowing dust sifted around her.

Pate pointed at a nest of twisted grasses. She gripped his hand tightly, and they crossed the threshold together. When they reached the grassy spot, he knelt and she settled beside him.

"Is something wrong?" Pate said.

She met his gaze. He could sense her hesitation.

"Caaqi brings change," Jema said, remembering Hunu's words.

Pate drew his jersey over his head. "Some find love," he nodded. "Some lose their senses."

Jema let him unbutton her shirt. "He's here in the jungle. Watching us."

Pate touched her sternum. He smoothed his fingers over her shoulder.

"He's more than a bird," Pate said. "He was circling over the stream where I caught the eels." He drew her gaze to the trumpet blooms, then he kissed her cheek.

His gentleness calmed her.

They lay down, and pencils of light beamed into the bower. One of them ticked across Pate's brow, making time slow. But though time seemed to lag, Jema's heart beat faster. Above them, the mouths of the trumpets flared and the golden dust was drifting down. And then Pate's eye was giant and close.

Jema held her breath.

Light was dripping from the ovate leaves, slowly, like oil. The trumpet fragrance was suddenly strong, from the heat of the day or because the pollen was thick. Could the magenta blooms feel her desire? Could they hear Pate whispering to the magenta inside her?

There was nothing to fear. Jema felt that surely. Faith in Pate filled her heart. She was held in warm, irresistible arms. Love embraced her, raw and overpowering. The boy you were meant for, the one you needed, the one you can't stay away from and can't live without—

A scream close by. Jema froze.

He's found us, she thought.

She could hear the beat of his wings, then over Pate's shoulder she saw him, swooping beneath the roroa crowns.

He showed his chocolate back as he banked, circling the clearing, head turned down. Come from a distance—

Pate had paused. "I'm here," he whispered.

The great parrot broke out of his circle, tilting and gliding toward them: two cockles and a cusp, his brows and nose; fog streaming back from his crown; wing fingers strafing the moss and the moldering soil.

Caaqi heeled abruptly, underwings flashing red through the winking pollen, settling on a branch above them—cheeks gold, dark widow's peak, black eyes peering down.

"Ready," the parrot said in a crackling voice—a rendition

of Hunu played on an old phonograph. He rattled his wings, epaulettes bristling. Then he fixed on Jema, and his black eyes hatched; in their depths she saw stars and glittering spokes, and his violent nature came boiling through, filling the space between them.

Pride, rage, passion, necessity— While Caaqi squawked and screeched, the frame of leaves around him shifted forward and back, as if about to consume her. Then, with a loud *cuck*, his thoughts emerged like the seed at the center of a nut that's been cracked.

She heard Caaqi speaking to her, speaking as the Governor might. As literate as her father, and his tone was as lofty. But his words were strange, so very strange.

Tricks and temptations, traps and lies— All the sly poisons and the brutal ones too: the degraded, the lewd, the maimed and useless; and the envied prize, my reward for the victors. Jema—

The Great Caaqi's eyes pinned and dilated. He can sense my feelings, she thought. He can read my mind, feel my desires.

All this will be yours, very soon. For the fearless: no craving held back, not a covet passed by. For the fearful: shock and dismay. Look, look— You can see them hiding, watching from loop and crevice: nightmare-rooted, eyes of doom, faces of jungle rubber, crooked and stretching.

What was the wild parrot telling her?

Pate's chest was heaving. He gasped in her ear. His whole body was clenching.

Caaqi whooped and whistled and beat his wings, then he

87

burst into cackles as if recalling a joke.

Pate bit her neck and hid his face in her shoulder. His breath, no longer a fury, began to slow.

What have you done? Jema thought.

She put her arms around Pate and met Caaqi's stare.

Who are you? she said.

The parrot didn't reply.

What's in our future? Jema insisted.

Caaqi spread his wings. *Chaos,* he answered. *Disorder and strife. Mobs and murders. Bloodshed and war.*

Our lives will be threatened, Jema thought.

They will, Caaqi replied.

You're frightening me, Jema thought. *Why are you saying these things? I'm just a kid.*

Not anymore, Caaqi said.

With that, he launched himself into the air. Jema saw the scarlet beat and felt the crazed bird trail his claws through her hair.

It was dusk when Jema woke. She opened her eyes, and Pate was beside her.

The terror of Caaqi's presence was still with her. She wondered how much of what she'd heard and felt had been real.

Jema sat up. There was a smear of blood on her thigh. She put her fingers to it, feeling the wetness.

Pate knelt beside her in the dimness, retrieving his clothing. Things seemed different, but not in a way she expected. He touched her once, twice, maintaining the link between them. But as he drew his pants on, he said little. Like he was having a conversation in secret with someone else.

She gathered her garments and dressed herself. Then she rose, dizzy, unsteady. Neither regret nor shame troubled her, but she felt cheated. Why had Caaqi appeared when he did? In the midst of love, what need was there of a message so dire?

Pate edged closer. He had two chocolate feathers in his hand, tokens the parrot had left behind. He tied them to the haft of his spear below the blade. Then they stepped out of the bower together and started back.

When they'd crossed the viaduct bridge, Jema paused and turned. The canyon was in shadow now, and so was the grove and the clearing. The bower of trumpets was barely visible, a passageway through the eye of a needle.

Pate reached for her hand. She saw the affection in his eyes, but it did little to allay her dismay and confusion. Why had Caaqi brought pleasure for him and dark prophecies for her? She wanted to share the parrot's inscrutable words, but they were jumbled and fading.

"Did you hear Caaqi speak?" she asked.

He looked up, scanning the canopy. Did he think the parrot was following them?

Pate said, "I heard him screaming."

He had satisfied his desire, Jema thought.

"Are you my wife now?"

She didn't know how to answer his question. "We can't tell anyone," she said.

Pate seemed uncertain whether she was talking about what they had done or the appearance of Caaqi.

When they reached the camp's border, he halted.

"There's hunting to do," he said.

She nodded. It was hard not to cry.

He kissed her goodbye, and she stood there watching until he'd disappeared through the trees.

As she approached the branch-and-vine shelters, she pictured herself high above, looking down. She saw a young woman approaching others, hesitant, torn, unsure if she still belonged to the clan. She wished she could tell Kris what had happened, but it was easy to imagine the resentment her friend might feel. And Ry-Lynn and Beth and Dee—certainly not. None of them would understand. Would they sense her mood and guess what she'd done?

That night, Jema dreamt of her father. She was living in the villa, and the Governor had never left. He watched her grow older, but he himself didn't age. Years passed, many years, until Jema was as old as he was. Old and wise. And as she aged, the Governor's speech slowed and his movements too, until finally he was perfectly still, frozen in time, turned to porcelain like the casting Kris took from her mother's boudoir.

The next morning, Jema woke with a strange conviction: her parents weren't coming back.

Pate's eel hunting continued, and the life of the camp began to circle around that. He delivered animals to Beth who carved them up. Rodney and Snugg harvested what they could from the forest and surviving gardens. Brice and his sister cooked and Venus served. After each meal, Dee cleaned up. Was she sampling the scraps? She wasn't eating with the rest of them.

In the evening, their erstwhile leader would retire to his shelter. Jema and the rest saw Venus carrying food to him—two skewers of roasted eel on a bed of leaves with fawn bread and clack nuts. Her steps had a bit of pomp, and she wore a solemn look. She would kneel at the entrance to Rangi's hut and call to him. A hand would emerge through the hanging vines, and she'd pass his dinner in. Her behavior incensed Kris, who seemed unaware that Venus was emulating her servility. Venus competed openly now for Rangi's attention, acting stupid and incapable around him. Jema tried to calm Kris, but Kris wouldn't have any of it. There was too much humiliation for her to admit to.

All of the kids showed their immaturity by taking Pate and the eels for granted.

With the need for nourishment met, Rangi's interest in survival waned, and the disregard spread to the other boys. When he wasn't inciting some contest in the woods, their leader was driving the Royal Express.

The train had practical functions. The circuit it made through the orchards and gardens allowed them to move their paltry harvest closer to camp. But increasingly, it was used for sport. The boys competed for the privilege of stoking the firebox. It was supposed to be loaded half full, but Rangi had them pack it to the top so the loco ran red hot. The girls could hear the whistle screaming and see the train careening through the trees.

One evening when the boys were late to return, Ry-Lynn said what Jema and others had been thinking. "That's not work."

"They're acting like fools," Kris agreed.

"What will happen," Dee said, "if they get hurt?"

When the boys returned to camp, Kris confronted Rangi. "The train isn't a toy," she said.

Rangi raised his hand and combed his fingers through his hair, as if to show her how luxurious it was. She waited for him to speak, but the silence drew out.

"No more joyrides," Kris said.

"You know better than that," Dee chimed in, speaking to Wyatt.

Jema saw Wyatt's lips purse. He looked troubled. He had been a good student. She'd sat next to him in class, and she respected him.

Wyatt faced Rangi. "The Governor had rules."

Rangi smiled. "Are you going to tell on us?"

The boys found that funny, and so did Venus.

Wyatt blushed and looked down. Jema felt his defeat, and

with it the defeat of Kris and the girls. Would things have gone differently if Pate had been present?

Snugg's scruffy stubble was filling in. Pate had a beard now, and so did Wyatt and Rodney. The dark mat on Rangi's face made his skin seem darker, and he looked like he'd grown in size: his shoulders were thicker, his chest wider, his jaw more pronounced. When they were children, Jema had never feared him, but things had changed. Rangi was a man now, and he had a new meanness.

She was thinking of this as she helped Ry-Lynn cut the early spring greens. When she looked up, she saw Beth and Venus running toward them.

"We were with Melody," Beth said, "in the forest, gathering firewood."

A chill rose up Jema's spine.

"She was between us," Venus explained. "We turned away and—"

"The ferns were over our knees," Beth said. "We thought she was playing with her doll or taking a nap."

Kris and Ry-Lynn hurried forward with Dee behind. Rangi and the boys saw the girls gathering and headed toward them. At the same time, Pate emerged from the forest, wearing a packboard with eels strapped to it. When Jema raised her arm, he read her urgency, unslung his burden and sped down the path, spear in hand.

Rangi got the gist from Venus and addressed the group. "We'll walk in widening circles, calling her name," he said. "Where did she disappear?"

Beth and Venus looked at each other.

"We got lost," Beth confessed.

"I saw you leave camp," Pate said to her. "You were headed west. The terrain descends in that direction." He spoke gently, calmly. "Were you walking uphill?"

"I don't think so," Beth answered.

"We'll make a net to catch her," Pate said. "We'll spread out in a line."

Venus turned to their leader to see what he thought. Rangi shrugged.

"I'll be in the middle," Pate said. "Kris, take the left wing. Rangi, the right."

The girls followed Kris, while the boys aligned themselves on the opposite side. Then Pate motioned the group forward.

They walked slowly, calling. From her place between Kris and Dee, Jema saw one and another of them drop out of sight and reappear. Was Melody backed against a log or nestling in a hollow?

They entered a dark wood where the trees were immense. Their calls continued unanswered. Dee looked fearful. She was whispering Melody's name. Beyond the dark wood, the ground grew spongy. Water bled from the moss at every step.

Rodney halted and called for the others to join him. At first Jema thought he'd hurt himself, but as the group gathered around, she saw he was holding the warrior doll. Rodney handed it to Pate, as if the doll might hold clues only Pate could divine.

"She's getting tired," Jema guessed.

Pate broke from the group, walked a few paces and knelt. Jema followed him, and as she drew closer, Pate rose with a chocolate feather in his hand. He handed it over to her, and she eyed it carefully, touching the vanes with a trembling finger.

Pate met her gaze, then he lifted his face, and she did too, scanning the canopy. The day was ending, sparks of the declining sun winking through. The burning villa, Jema thought. The friction with Rangi. The tension in the camp mounting daily. It seemed that misfortune, having found them, was following them now like a wild animal that, having fed once, returns wanting more.

She looked at the feather. Please help us, she thought.

Pate was directing the group, re-forming the line. "Slower," he told them. "Keep together. If we don't find her by dark, we'll camp and start again at first light."

The sinuous line resumed its march. As they covered the ground, the night came to meet them.

"Here," Kris cried.

The twilight seemed to shine more brightly at her shout, then faded completely.

They all stumbled to where Kris was crouched at the edge of a stream.

Melody was curled on the bank, dirty and disheveled but unharmed, relieved to see them. They all spoke reassuring words to her. Pate handed her the doll, which she grabbed and held to her chest.

"Look at this," Ry-Lynn exclaimed.

She was standing by the stream bank, peering down. A swarm of eels was visible, holding steady in the current, their undulating backs above the surface, teeth glowing silver. Jema looked up. A crescent moon had appeared through a break in the canopy, and on the limb of a tree high above the stream, she saw a familiar silhouette. Melody was by Jema's leg. As Jema lifted the little girl in her arms, Caaqi spread his wings and departed.

"Why did you leave?" Jema whispered.

Melody's lips trembled. "I want my mommy."

Jema sobbed despite herself, hugging the little girl. "I'm your mommy now."

Pate led the group back through the forest. He halted in a glade where giant sword ferns grew. He told them they would sleep beneath the ferns in case it rained, and the group made beds in the loam as he directed. Jema stretched out facing him, with Melody between them.

4

While Pate was gone, hunting for eels, Jema noticed a change in the behavior of the girls. They stopped talking or changed the subject when she approached. Unexpectedly, Dee sidled up and spoke to her in a prying way. Were rumors circulating? Then just before dinner one night, Ry-Lynn confirmed Jema's fears. Kris was standing, listening.

"We know what you're doing with Pate," Ry-Lynn said. "Everyone does, even Venus."

How had they been found out?

"That's so scrubby," Kris said.

"You're jealous," Jema shot back. "If Rangi—"

But before she could finish, the two girls were stepping away.

That night, when she lay down beside Kris, her old friend turned her back to her. And as soon as she closed her eyes, Caaqi began to trill. Was he trying to warn her? Did he mean to shame her, like Kris and Ry-Lynn? Was he venting some inhuman desire, some fractious need she could not comprehend?

The trills came from the woods behind the shelter. Jema rose, or dreamt that she rose, and stepped outside. In the moonlight, she saw Caaqi hanging from a branch, holding on with one foot while he sang. As she drew closer he let himself go, batting through the air two feet from the ground. He hovered beside her, goading her, urging her— To do what?

Then Caaqi flapped up before her, grabbed her shirt with his claws and beak, and shook her, wrenching her close and thrusting her back. Wrathful, she thought. Incensed on her behalf. Or angry with her, trying to stir a conflict to life.

When Jema woke the next morning, she discovered that no one had heard Caaqi but her. They'd finished dressing when Rangi showed up at their hut carrying empty buckets. He asked Kris if she and the girls would help him fetch water. In retrospect, Jema realized how false the request was. He'd never done that before. He viewed the chore as beneath his dignity.

Kris was harsh. "Do it yourself."

Rangi pleaded with her. "Come on. Help me out."

"Ask Venus," Kris said.

Rangi shook his head. "I want you."

Jema hoped for Kris' sake that his winking interest was real. Kris relented, Ry-Lynn and Dee joined them, and the five set off for the stream.

Rangi sagged to the rear and fell slowly behind. When Jema turned to see what was holding him up, he dropped the pails and reached into his pants. An odd expression livened his face—not fear, not joy, but something closer to pain, as if a spider had bitten his male parts and he was trying to remove it.

The others stopped too, and the four girls stood watching as Rangi pulled his weapon out. It wasn't limp. It was stiff, and he waved it with a menacing scowl.

Jema struggled to guess what he had in his head. Was he trying to frighten them with the sight? Was he thinking of using the weapon on them?

Assuming the more innocent motive, Jema put her back to Rangi and clutched Venus' arm to turn her away. Kris had a different reaction. She stood watching Rangi, waiting to see what more he intended.

Venus was wide-eyed. "Why—"

"Who can tell," Jema said.

"What is she doing?" Ry-Lynn murmured.

When Jema turned to look, Kris was striding toward Rangi. "Alright," she snarled and motioned him toward her, daring him. Smiling, or smirking rather, returning the threat in a strange way.

Rangi let go of his weapon, and a cruel laugh rose in his throat. Jema could see the gleam in his eyes, and she knew in an instant: Kris was his target. She must be frightened, Jema thought. She must be.

But Kris was reaching her hands toward Rangi's groin, calling his bluff.

Dee gasped. Ry-Lynn's jaw quivered.

"Give me that thing," Kris said.

Rangi laughed and tucked his weapon back in his pants. Then he turned and retreated back down the trail.

The girls returned to camp single file behind Kris.

Word spread quickly. Beth came to Jema to ask what had happened, having heard a salacious version from Brice. The boys were saying that Jema and Ry-Lynn had been tempted. Kris responded with derision. "He doesn't know what to do with it," she said.

Jema wondered if Rangi had any real feelings for Kris, or if his behavior had been triggered by the rumors about her and Pate. Maybe Rangi just wanted to steal the show. The flagrant act was making him a celebrity. The girls jabbered and tittered about it, while the boys showed their dash by embellishing the story.

Jema longed for Pate, but finding eels took time. He might be absent for days. Without him, who would have the confidence to challenge Rangi? They were on their own in the jungle, without judge or court or parental authority. There was only group favor and disapproval. Rodney and Snugg were impressed by what Rangi had done. Wyatt was amused. Venus, instead of being horrified, seemed fascinated. And Brice had new information, which he shared with his sister: Wyatt wanted to have sex with Ry-Lynn, and Ry-Lynn had agreed. But Ry-Lynn knew nothing about it.

"They're not men," Kris laughed. "They're all like Rangi. All they can do is wave it around."

"I'm scared," Dee confessed.

"He looked at me," Venus explained, "when he aimed his cack."

"'Cack?'"

"That's what you call it," Venus nodded, as if she knew. There was awe in her eyes, and more than a little pride. "Rangi likes me."

Uncertainty ruled the camp for two days. And then Rangi made an announcement at dinner. He stood by the pit, with the fire behind him, and scanned the group.

"Kris and I are going to have sex," he said.

No one spoke. Kris stirred the leaves between her feet.

"On the train," Rangi said, "at high speed."

Beth and Brice removed the skewers of eel meat from the flames and passed them around. The group ate without a word being spoken.

Later that night, in their shelter, Jema pressed Kris.

"You're not going to do it, are you?"

Kris looked past her, eyes turned to slits. "He doesn't frighten me."

This is a dare, Jema thought, not a gesture of love. Kris was like Rangi in her recklessness. Then Kris met her gaze, and all the wariness and suspicion between them was gone. They were friends again. Best friends. It seemed the attention Rangi had given her had restored Kris' power and self-esteem.

"He's taking Rodney to stoke the firebox," Kris said. "I want you there."

Jema shook her head. Was this Rangi's idea?

"Please," Kris said.

"I used to trust Rangi. I don't anymore."

"It'll be a big nothing," Kris laughed. "He doesn't have the nerve."

In the end, for friendship, despite her better judgment, Jema agreed.

The next morning, the four of them boarded the loco—Rangi at the throttle, Kris beside him, Rodney stoking the firebox, Jema kneeling two feet away. She handed sectioned logs to Rodney, hearing the puff of the engine and the *clack* of the wheels on the rail joints as they passed the gardens and orchards.

Rangi foiled her fears. He focused on his driving duties, looking fondly at Kris from time to time. He seemed like the boy he'd once been: not always maligned, not always defiant. His eyes weren't hooded, they were wide and clear.

The train wound down the slope, skirting a curved embankment reinforced with wine bottles, all planted under the Governor's supervision, neck-in. They passed the wood-cutter's shed, where branches sleeved with moss were piled beside rotting stumps, and the Soprano's Gullet appeared ahead. Was Kris right? Was this all for show, for the rest of the band?

Sex on the train, even with a willing partner, would be a challenge. You could stop the loco and lie down—on a flat car perhaps, or in a glade near the tracks. Then, as they approached the tunnel, Jema thought: you could pause the train in the dark interior. But the loco didn't slow. They emerged from the Gullet's far end and started up a steep grade, chugging slowly.

Rangi took one hand off the controls and motioned to Kris to get down on her knees. She laughed.

Rangi motioned again, gently, with a beseeching look.

"You'll have to beg," Kris said.

"Please," Rangi said, "please, please. Do it for them, for us, for me. We are the leaders, king and queen. Kris—this is how it should be."

He unfastened his pants and tugged them down.

Rodney looked away. Jema watched her friend.

Kris wore a crooked smile. She nodded to show she understood but had no intention of lowering herself to do his bidding.

Rangi took his hands off the controls and opened his arms. "I love you, Kris."

In a heartbeat, all unexpected, Kris gasped and fell to her knees, hands reaching for Rangi's thighs. Jema saw the flash of pride and triumph in Rangi's face. Then he looked at Rodney, roared, smacked Kris away and pulled his pants up.

Kris rolled onto her side, crushed and sobbing, curling on the loco grating.

Jema was stunned and speechless. She sank, crawling beside her friend, hugging her, holding her close as Rangi drove the Royal Express back down the ridge.

In their shelter, Kris cried her heart out, unable to believe that Rangi had done what he'd done for no other reason than to humiliate her. She was a fool, Jema thought, to make Rangi the keeper of her happiness. But Jema knew she was doing the same with Pate. Judgment and faith—that was all a young woman had.

"We'll be okay," she said, trying to reassure Kris and herself.

A moment later, the other girls were crowding inside the shelter.

Ry-Lynn knelt and embraced Kris, and the rest huddled close, holding each other, imagining their combined body might be large enough to absorb the sorrow.

"He doesn't care about you," Ry-Lynn said.

"Everyone knows," Dee muttered. "Rodney's his witness."

"He did it to hurt you." Beth looked at Jema. "To tear you down."

A moment of silence as the girls thought about this. The depths of Rangi's deceit astonished them.

"There's more," Ry-Lynn said quietly. She glanced at Beth.

"Brice played the same stunt as Rangi on the trail," Ry-Lynn said. "He showed Dee his cack."

Dee gave a mortified laugh and nodded.

"Did it look like Rangi's?" Venus asked.

"Smaller," Dee said. "Hard to see. It was all shriveled up."

"I'm sorry," Kris mewled. "I'm so, so sorry."

Pate appeared at twilight that evening with a packboard

of eels. As Jema helped him unstrap his catch, she explained what had happened.

"Rangi—" Pate looked aside, muffling his contempt. "He's a nest of thorns."

Jema heard, in his voice, years of gall and provocation. No one knew Rangi better.

"His care for Kris was never real."

A few minutes later, kids were collecting around the fire-pit. As soon as Rangi sat down, Pate strode up to him.

"Leave the girls alone," Pate said, "and stay away from Jema."

Rangi returned a cold stare. There was more than scorn or dismissal in it. Jema saw a grinding resentment.

The other boys approached, swaggering, standing on either side of their leader. An air of testy amusement infected the group. Rodney and Snugg traded mirthful words. Wyatt looked complicit with Rangi's disdain. Was he the older boy's henchman now? Beth glared at Brice, who was sniggering with the rest.

Kris emerged from the dimness and stepped to the fire-pit rim, opposite Rangi. She closed her eyes, aware she was at the drama's center but needing for a moment to blind herself. Then she placed her hands over her ears and shook her head violently, as if she was trying to purge the voices and words. The girls tensed as one, contracting like a muscle around her. Jema saw Melody hurrying forward. She lifted the little girl up, holding her close.

With a shriek and thrashing of fists, Kris exploded at Rangi.

"I should have expected cruelty from a motherless cannibal." She spread her scorn to the boys who flanked him.

"No one's bowing to you anymore," Rangi sneered. Then to the boys, "She's the one on her knees." At that, Rodney laughed and Snugg tittered.

"Monsters," Ry-Lynn cried out.

"We're men," Wyatt answered her sternly.

"You're supposed to honey us up," Snugg griped.

Jema was stunned, Dee speechless, Beth confused. Where did this indignation come from? Had Rangi been nursing it all the while?

"We're done eating together," Kris said. "Maybe we'll live apart too."

The words shocked Jema. She shuddered, checking her sisters. They looked startled and stiff, but roused by Kris' resistance. It was like one of the spats they'd read about in the magazines. They were crossing the border, Jema thought, between a civilized life, like the one their parents led, and a frightening life that none were prepared for.

"This is our village," Ry-Lynn told the boys, extending her arm toward the branch-and-vine homes.

"No it's not," Wyatt replied.

"The shelters were my idea," Ry-Lynn insisted.

"Keep them," Rangi said. "We'll live in the wilds. We're taking the tools from the butcher shed."

"They belong to us," Snugg shouted. "Rodney found them."

"And the grills," Rangi said.

"I need them to cook," Beth told Kris.

"You can't stop us," Rodney said, retrieving a sack from the woodpile. He began putting knives and grilling forks in it.

Pate was staring at Jema. She stared back, shaking her head.

"The train is ours," Rangi proclaimed.

"My father built it," Jema objected.

"You can have the train," Kris told Rangi. "We're keeping the orchards and gardens."

"And your mom's clothes," Venus added.

"We'll make our home," Rangi faced the boys, "on the native side of the ridge. What do you say? No girls allowed."

Wyatt blinked. Snugg looked at Rodney.

"We're staying here," Kris answered, "on the civilized side."

Jema thought, What comfort was that? She looked from Venus to Brice, from Wyatt to Dee, seeing how the prospect of dividing was frightening them all.

"I'm going to stay with my sister," Brice muttered.

"You're coming with us," Rangi said. "You're the cook." He faced Pate. "What about you?"

That silenced both sides. The tribe had survived thanks to Pate's hunting.

"Will you go with us or the girls?" Rangi demanded.

Jema looked at Pate, fearful the split would uncouple them.

"No boys are going to live in this camp," Kris declared.

Rangi nodded. "Then he's coming with us."

Pate faced Rangi. "I'll find my own shelter. And I'll take Jema with me."

"Are you serious?" Wyatt said.

"Can he do that?" Snugg looked at Rodney.

Melody wrapped her arms around Jema's legs.

What was Pate thinking? she wondered.

Jema hoped the vicious exchange might be set aside. But Kris and Rangi had made up their minds, and the rest had no choice but to follow. So with a minimum of words the scavengings were divided, along with eel meat and the stored produce. Rodney loaded sacks full of tools and blades. Brice strapped blankets and grills to his packboard. Wyatt packed up their share of the food.

When the boys were ready to depart, Kris posted herself on the trail at their rear. "Don't come back," she told Rangi.

He returned her glare. "Stay out of our way."

Pate remained in the camp, while Jema pleaded with Kris.

"He's been good to us," she said. "He's fed us. He's not like Rangi."

"No," Kris said. "No boys."

"What are we going to eat?"

"We'll get our own eels." Kris put her hand on Jema's shoulder. "You can't leave your sisters or Melody or me." She spoke with a tenderness that came from their past.

Jema nodded. She couldn't. She and Kris were best friends. But it didn't seem right that she should have to choose.

An hour later, Jema and Melody accompanied Pate to the camp's border. "Come with me," he had begged her, and she'd explained why she couldn't. But she was feeling the hurt of losing him now, a hurt that was more than mere separation.

"Where will you sleep tonight?" she asked him.

"I'll find a spot."

"How will you survive on your own?"

"I don't know," Pate said. "I'll figure it out."

If she wanted to see him, what would she do? There was no way for them to speak to each other. Time was still behind her, Jema thought. But it was moving fast, about to pass through her, to pass through them both. If love didn't get their full attention, it might be lost. It would forget them and focus on others, like a restless hunter searching for game.

Pate lifted Melody up, hugged her and kissed her cheeks, then set her back down.

Jema smiled a sad smile, and the two of them waved as Pate continued along the trail. He paused by a boulder and waved his goodbye, but with far less concern. He'd been an orphan, she thought, and he was still unsure there was a home for him, even in the heart of another.

Pate managed, and so did she. Nine days passed before Jema saw him again, but when he appeared in camp, he was in good spirits, fit and healthy. He told her of a temporary hut he'd built, and of a new technique he'd devised for catching eels by luring them into pens by the side of a stream.

The girls didn't take up hunting, and neither did the boys. Pate caught his eels and delivered them to both tribes, bartering for things he needed. He reported, as well, on each to the other when there was news.

The boys made their own camp in a depression at the terminus of the train loop. "They've strung hammocks in a shady grove," Pate said. "They're getting drunk on kohu." Kohu was a wild squash. The rind was tough and the pulp inedible; but when ripe, the squash produced a golden juice and when overripe, fermentation occurred. "The place is a mess," Pate said, "bedstraw and eel guts everywhere. They spend most of their time riding the train, climbing trees and swinging from vines."

On his visits, he told Jema of his trials and triumphs, of the flaws in his temporary hut, and of a more permanent one underway. He reassured her that he was safe, but as soon as he left, her fears would return. When she paused in her work to think about him, her heart seemed to fall, not as with a burden but with a weightless descent, the way a bird pushing off a high limb would fall before catching a draft. She spoke to him in the late hours, imagining her words reached him while he slept or as he padded through the moonlit jungle.

In the second month, after a week of waiting for him, Jema took matters into her own hands. She left Melody in Beth's care and followed the trail Pate had marked. When she arrived, she received a new kind of welcome. The home he was building was in the trees, above ground. The first platform had been laid, and when the rains allowed, they slept there on a mattress of leaves.

Between hunting eels and building the Treehouse, Pate never stopped working. While she was there, Jema worked with him. Pate had found a stand of Caaqi's Breath not far from the Treehouse. He'd collected some trumpet pollen, he said. He'd sampled the Breath and summoned the parrot, getting "guidance" from him—advice that puzzled Jema and troubled her too.

"He speaks to you?" she said.

"I can hear what Caaqi is thinking," Pate replied. "He's encouraging me."

"To do what?"

"Explore, learn. To find my own way in the jungle."

His own way. Was Caaqi reinforcing Pate's insularity?

"He may have plans for us," Pate said.

Plans? What kind of plans?

Her last night with Pate, they inhaled the Breath together. He took a pinch and raised it to his lips. The candlelight trembled, and Pate blew a puff of pollen at her. Jema felt it on her lashes and in her nostrils as she drew it in. The Breath was like casting off, leaving by boat on a long journey.

Then Caaqi descended, and instead of frightening her, the great parrot reached with his claws and gripped them both, crushing their hearts and fusing them, so that the current that bore them away held them perfectly together. In Caaqi's grasp, Jema's fears vanished. A sense of promise overcame her, a joy and sureness she'd never felt. Naked and selfless, with Caaqi around them, there could be no doubt, no pause, no question. It was not at all like that first time in the arbor.

On her return to the girls' camp, Kris made a scene. With the girls gathered round, Kris accused her of abandoning them. It was as if Jema's gladness had opened her to a new kind of pain. She begged for Kris' forgiveness, but Kris' outlook on boys had been poisoned by Rangi. Their friendship was coiled with envy now.

What could Jema do? She ignored Kris' reproaches. She snuck away to spend time with Pate whenever she could find someone to watch Melody. The trysts grew longer. Every day with Pate yielded its fruit, and the accrual of days built gradually to something more powerfully sweet than the sum of its parts. They were changing, and quickly. Pate's voice deepened. His confidence grew, along with his skill in meeting the jungle's challenges. Under her eyes, he was becoming a man, with a man's forthrightness and gravity. And under his eyes she was becoming a woman. Her monthly bleeding halted. She felt queasy and her breasts were tender. They both knew what that meant.

Jema helped pen the eels, string the vine ladders to the

Treehouse, frame the window openings with branches, impressed by the new Pate while recalling the old one fondly. When she was with the girls and he appeared with his eels, her admiration soared. At the outset, the girls had wild harvests and provisions to share. But as their stores dwindled, Pate bartered for containers and towels and tools—things to fit out the Treehouse. Melody went running to greet him as she once ran to greet her father.

Kris accepted Pate in his role as hunter, but the dependency rankled her and fed her jealousy and resentment of Jema. And Kris' bitterness spread to the other girls. At each return to the camp, Jema became more aware of it. Emotions flared. One's distress infected another, mounting and spreading. On occasions the upset approached hysteria. The girls clung desperately to each other, then suddenly they'd turn vicious or tearful.

Hatred for the boys mounted. In that, they all followed Kris. Ry-Lynn's disdain was dressed in content. "We're so much happier now," she crowed. As Dee starved and dwindled, her boy-gall mounted. Beth now counted herself Pate's equal—she'd become a hunter and had managed to trap a few birds.

Kris nursed a special animosity for Venus, because of her youth or her adulation of Rangi.

"Who named you?" Kris demanded.

The younger girl quailed.

"Your father, I bet," Kris said with contempt.

Venus looked surprised. "You just guessed."

"Only a man could be that cruel," Kris said. "Look in the mirror."

The upset spawned delusions. Dee said she'd been awakened in the night by the boys' drunken hootings. On a visit to the latrine, Beth saw their silhouettes dancing through the trees.

One evening in their shelter, Kris attacked Pate.

"He doesn't care about you," Kris said.

Jema looked away.

"He's going to break your heart," Kris said. "You'll come crawling back, begging me to pick up the pieces."

Pate stood knee-deep in the stream, his whetted spear raised, ready to strike. His tanned chest was dappled with golden coins that shifted as a breeze moved the boughs above. Through the patterns, Jema saw his frame tense. His muscled arm swelled and drove the spear through the head of an eel.

He let go of the spear, grabbed the eel with both hands and lifted it out of the water. Jema darted beneath and got hold of the slimy middle. The black eel arched and bent, winding its tail around her legs, while the seeking nose flexed in the air around Pate's head.

He hurled the eel onto the bank, pulled a knife from his belt and sawed at its neck. The body whipped, coiling in on itself, trying to find some recovery within. Jema held on. She could feel the black creature spasm and soften. Then it was still.

Pate stood in the sun, knife blade dripping. After months in the wild, on the path to manhood, Pate had hardened. He was covered with eel slime, and so was she. He dropped the knife, closed the distance and helped her up, and they waded into the stream together.

Jema's foot slid on the mossy stones, and she fell with a splash. She shrieked, feeling the thick bodies of the eels gliding past as Pate slid beside her, smiling, while he washed the slime off her arms. His hair was longer, the brown gilded by sun. She put her lips to his, and for a moment she imagined they were eels too, carried downstream, set writhing by the current.

When the kiss ended, she opened her eyes. Pate was looking at her in a way he never had before—as if he didn't know her but loved what he saw.

They rose together and returned to the dead eel. Pate looped the vine harness behind its fins, head half-detached. They started downstream, dragging the beast. Then up the opposite bank, ascending a slope till they reached the root wheel of a giant fallen roroa. Beside it was a second giant, still standing.

In toppling over—how loud the sound must have been—the space where the roots were was a pit now. "The Boggy Pit" they called it, and it was there Pate collected the eels he'd slain. They lifted the recent catch over the rim and watched as its black body sank, joining others. How many, it was hard to tell, as they were coiled together beneath the water, like creatures secured behind glass in the capital's history museum. The only head visible, Jema saw, belonged to the recent addition. Its unblinking eyes watched her, and the flat, inscrutable gaze gave neither counsel nor judgment.

Four months had passed since Pate left the others, and Jema's stays had grown longer. With the summer heat, the afternoon rains returned, but the Treehouse had a roof now. It was dry in the waking hours, and they could sleep there at night. With the day's catch in the Pit, they headed home now, walking in silence side by side. Jema put her hand on her middle, imagining the new life growing beneath. They passed through columns of afternoon sun, hit a trail that mounted a slope and entered a dense grove, losing their dapples and stripes. The shade changed them, it seemed, into different beings: darker, graver, more earnest, more knowing of each other.

The grove ended at the maruna thickets. As they wound through them, Jema passed her hands over the leaves. At night, the maruna were luminous. When you stirred the leaves, a golden line pulsed down the spine of each. Now and then, in the middle of the night, you could see the path of an animal moving through it. Or if the wind was strong enough, you could see it passing like a comb through hair.

It was because of the stream, the maruna's magic, and the waterfall farther up that Pate had located the Treehouse here.

It came into view, built between two immense roroas,

thirty feet up and held by their branches. Pate grabbed the vine ladder and began his ascent. Jema followed.

Halfway up, the cascade appeared, its white cords and foam painting the cliff behind. The spray caught in their hair in sparkling droplets.

Behind the watery sheet, those who'd once lived by the fall had etched images into the rock. The petroglyphs, faint at midday, grew more visible when the sidelong light of sundown or dawn brought them back to the surface. A rank of warriors stood holding the detached heads of those they'd slain. The warriors' eyes bulged, and so did the eyes of the dead.

As they reached the top of the ladder, the Treehouse appeared before them. Pate gripped the post above the mooring and swung through the wedge-shaped entrance. Jema followed.

There were windows everywhere, framed by branches— odd-shaped openings without panes. The floor had many levels, wherever the trees' basal arms allowed boughs to be laid. A bed made of knobby stumps stood above a plank table where either could work, and where they left notes to each other using a technique Pate devised. There was a rubbery creeper called panghi rope, and if you drilled a hole in the rope, it would bleed black sap that could be used as ink. With a twig for a pen, you could write a message on a kohu leaf and weight it on the table with a rock. The two of them traded notes often, while Pate came and went, hunting.

Beside the table was shelving, and on the shelf were books

with scorched covers. They had returned to the ruins of Jema's villa and found them in a burnt chest at the back of the Governor's study. The volumes were time-limited and therefore precious. The pages crumbled as you turned them. Some could be read only once.

Melody was seated on the floor by the table, chewing clack nuts while she scribed her name on a roroa root. She ran to greet them. "We're going to cover those chairs," Pate said, "with dry ferns." The frames were made of knobby boughs.

Melody smiled and nodded.

"She's happy here." Pate looked at Jema.

"She is," Jema agreed.

"You don't have to go back."

"Neither do you," she said.

"I trade with them." Pate shrugged.

"Is there anything they have that we need?" she asked.

Pate met her gaze with a searching look. "I don't want them to die. I still care about them."

"So do I," she said.

Hours later, when twilight descended, the long rays of the sun passed through the western openings, glazing the screen of woven vines behind which Melody slept.

Jema stood naked beside Pate, looking out over the maruna thickets. He had his arm around her waist and his lips to her ear.

"You're everything," he said.

Jema could hear the waterfall and feel the Treehouse trembling.

Pate seemed to be holding something in—some thought as yet unvoiced—uncertain whether he should share it.

"You're my wife now," he whispered. "Aren't you?"

"I am," she said. Wife. Parent to Melody. And the seedbed for their jungle child.

Pate faced her and brought their naked bodies together. She was still a bit nervous. Pate's desire always seemed urgent. She did all she could to calm herself, to open her heart and welcome him in. There was nothing about her life now that bore any resemblance to the life she had led a few months before.

"Ready?" Pate asked.

She nodded.

He opened his hand, using his fingers to spread the lips of the pouch he'd made from an eel's head. Then he took a pinch and held it between them. As she watched, he popped his thumb and forefinger, sending a puff of pollen into the air.

Pate inhaled, drawing the glitter in. Jema did the same.

The familiar dizziness gripped her. She faced the branch-framed opening and put her hands on the wood. The sun was sinking behind the hills, bathing her in orange light.

Pate began to whisper. As if from a distance, the familiar incitement sounded.

Caaq, caaq, caaqi. Was it in or outside her head? *Caaq, caaq, caaqi,* dividing her thoughts again and again.

A scream, and the Great Caaqi appeared on the far horizon. A small T at first, dark and flattened. Over the distant forest, the native side, the parrot came gliding.

Pate was behind her now.

Caaqi was speaking, speaking to them. Aspiring, warning, promising, his voice woven with shrieks, urgent, keen and consuming, swallowing everything.

Darkness closed behind him, the forest breathing, fronds lifting, large and small, lifting and dipping as one, honoring him, the ruler of nature.

Caaq, caaq, caaqi. Caaq, caaq, caaqi.

The sycophants bowed, sighing and scraping; and as before, the assailing presence—the jungle god and the ancient prostration—frightened her. The ideas she'd harbored and was still hanging on to—kinship and community, being in the care of adoring friends and protecting adults— Was it all a child's fantasy, worn-out and simpleminded?

A duff candle was burning behind them, and in the wavering light their shadows loomed and pulsed, the shadows of giants, yearning, expecting Caaqi's arrival. The pulse was mounting. Jema felt it surround and pervade her—a rhythmic beat, weighty and dense: the cadence of Caaqi's wings.

She gripped the sill, making fists of her hands. Pate's covered hers.

In a heartbeat, they were with the great bird, sweeping over the maruna, stirring the sleeping shrubs to life. Caaqi rasped in her ears, and the spines of the leaves glowed and came loose. A million golden needles floated beneath her. Jema heard whispers she could not understand, breathed scents, felt pressures, succumbing to pleasures— Everything around her seemed fresh and just-finished, as if it had, only a moment before, been released into the world.

My future's here, Jema thought, knowing Caaqi was listening.

Wings spread wide on a wild glide, the giant beak gaped and freed a curdling cry.

Caaqi agreed, but his fervor went beyond Pate and the Treehouse. The jungle's inhuman god wanted more—much more—than that.

Four large eels were strapped to Pate's packboard, heads skyward, swaying as he walked. Their nail-like teeth glittered in the sun.

The boys' camp was deep in the jungle, in what looked like a hollow that might have been occupied by natives in centuries past. Jema had asked to accompany Pate. He refused at first, but she had insisted. She wanted to see.

"On this soil, beneath these trees," Pate swept the foreground, "they beheaded each other."

Instead of a pale rock on the ground before her, Jema imagined a moss-covered skull. Pate sounded like Hunu, with his evocation of headhunting and cannibal feasts.

"They're still here," he said, "woven into the roots of these giants."

Jema could imagine the skulls, scattered beneath the

surface—an unending array, a vast underground constellation on the roof of which the living walked.

"Rangi's taste for kohu has no limits," Pate said. "They're drunk night and day."

She had heard plenty about the deterioration of the boys' tribe. According to Pate, Rangi's tyranny was absolute. None of them dared disobey him. Rangi regularly beat up the boys for no other reason than to prove his fierceness. Pate's judgment fell harshly on Wyatt. According to Pate, Jema's old classmate had remade himself in Rangi's image. Not only did he bow to their twisted leader, Wyatt had absorbed his cruel spirit and lorded it over the other boys.

The Royal Express, in recent weeks, had become the site of status tests. They tied up Snugg and rode him around on a flat car; and when they reached the viaduct bridge, they hung him over the gorge. The train was now a symbol of dominion over the jungle, and loco courage was an arbiter of rank.

As they approached the camp, Jema saw corridors of trampled brush divided by offal dumps and ash heaps. Pate followed the footpath to a stand of trees, and when he turned to look at her, Jema understood. We're not part of this, he seemed to say.

He left her by the gnarled roots of a tall roroa and tramped toward the center of camp. She could see a smoldering fire, vine hammocks with giant fern fronds suspended above them to keep off the rains.

Boys appeared through the woods. Some wore kilts of leaves. Their hair was long. Instead of cutting it, they had tied it behind. They approached Pate. Jema saw him unshoulder his packboard and unstrap the eels.

A clot of boys milled around him, then Wyatt and Rodney began hauling the meat to another location. Brice and Snugg spoke to Pate. Jema couldn't hear what was said, but she saw Pate turn and point, and the boys' eyes followed, seeing her standing beside the tree.

For a few moments, they seemed to be talking about her. Brice waved, and Jema waved back. In the first few months, Pate had explained, Rodney and Brice resisted the descent into savagery. Brice, more than the rest, clung to the hope that the childhood they'd known would somehow return. But the hopes had fled. All they had now was the thrill of freedom and the fear of what might befall them through conflicts, accidents or reckless behavior.

As Pate mingled with the boys, Jema realized how un-like them he was. Self-sufficient, independent—he seemed so much older. The need for inclusion, the need for acceptance— It was nothing to Pate. Would any of them ever be like him?

Then Rangi appeared.

He strode through the undergrowth, raising his arms, clapping Pate on the back, hugging him. Then Rangi turned, a beam of sun struck his face, and Jema saw what had been done to it. Nothing Pate said had prepared her. It wasn't a boy's face. It belonged in the jungle.

Wyatt had traced a pattern, Pate said. Then using a stick with a thorn, he had dipped the thorn into panghi ink, placed it on Rangi's face and struck it with a rock, driving the point in. The dark tattoo had tears of rage and a hateful grin. "I used to think it was just a show," Pate said, "but he's become the part he was playing."

Rangi's chest was bare and so were his legs. He was wearing a necklace of eel teeth. On his wrists and ankles were bands of braided hair. Jema couldn't hear what was said, but Rangi seemed to be promoting some idea to Pate.

"Why not?" he asked, giving Pate a wicked look.

Pate seemed noncommittal.

When Pate was done, he returned to the tree, and he and Jema started back.

"He wants a meeting with Kris," Pate said.

The next morning, Jema returned with Melody to the girls' camp.

As they drew near, they saw smoke and cinders spiraling up. The firepit came into view, and Ry-Lynn and Beth were seated beside it, thumbing through magazines. With the growth of the vines, the shelters behind them looked like green dust devils spinning beneath the trees.

Ry-Lynn looked up, Beth smiled at Melody, and for a moment Jema was struck. Both girls were unkempt, their faces grimy, hair greasy and shingled. Jema had only been gone for a few days. Had the girls been like this when she left?

Warm weather had made the roroa ears unusable for bathing. With the rise in temperature, the collected rain turned fetid, and the baths were humming with mosquitoes and crawling with newts. To get clean, you had to wash in the stream or throw off your clothes when a cloud burst—but it wasn't that hard.

Dee had put a blanket over the scorched mirror. She and Venus were distressed by how they looked, but the distress didn't change their behavior. They mocked each other and made things worse. There was still some discipline when it came to the tasks. But many of the girls' responsibilities were forgotten. Ry-Lynn spent much of her time pandering to Kris; the gardens were poorly tended, and the orchards too. They survived for the most part on eel meat, with herbs they found at the stream's edge and fawn bread pulled from the trees.

"When is Pate coming?" Beth asked.

"In three or four days," Jema replied.

Pate arrived on schedule.

After unloading his eels, he explained to Kris that there was something they needed to talk about, so she allowed him to stay for dinner.

They were seated around the fire, Kris next to Pate, Jema kneeling with Melody on the opposite side. The sky was overcast, the jungle cold and damp.

Beth handed Pate a steaming tin cup, then began passing bowls around. In Jema's, there was roasted eel meat and some greens, dark and withered. "Please," Beth said, trying to force food on Dee. "A few bites." Dee's shins were like branches and her thighs were gone.

Pate was speaking to Kris, looking earnest and concerned.

"He has nothing to trade?" Kris asked.

Pate shook his head. The girls had made things—utensils, leaf ponchos, shoe treads from tree bark—for barter. But all the boys' goods had been scavenged from the villas, and they'd already handed most of that over.

"How is my brother?" Beth asked.

"He burnt his arm feeding the loco," Pate replied.

The girls could hear the concern in his voice.

"A branch tore Rodney's shoulder open," Pate went on. "Swinging on vines."

"What a worthless lot they've become," Kris said.

"We can hear them," Ry-Lynn told Pate, "when the train crosses the bridge. Last week someone was screaming."

"That was Snugg," Pate said.

"Let them starve," Kris directed him, as if her command extended to Pate when he was in their territory.

He looked past the firepit into the trees. "He has them making weapons—pikes, clubs, blades with long handles."

Silence around the pit.

Finally Venus spoke. "What for?" she wondered.

But the others understood. Kris looked at Jema, suspecting this was information she knew.

"He doesn't scare me," Kris said loudly.

"Rangi asked me to deliver a message," Pate said. "He

wants a meeting. To talk about putting the tribes back together."

"So he can make us his slaves," Kris said.

"We could give them fawn bread," Melody suggested.

Jema put her hand on the little girl's shoulder and drew her closer.

"Is that all?" Kris said.

Pate sighed. "He asked me to tell you that he's sorry for what he did. 'We could have been like you and Jema.'"

Kris' lips parted. A caustic laugh emerged from her throat.

"He's not to be trusted," Pate said. "But it may make sense to talk before things get worse."

Kris rose, scanning the faces. "We won't be misled, misused or mistreated."

"We were better off," Jema said, "when we were all together."

"Where there is no trust," Kris glared at her, "there will be no recombining." She scanned the group. "Women are fools. My father had wealth and power, and he wasn't a savage. But Mother still had to drink herself stupid to take the abuse."

Kris pursed her lips and stepped toward the shelters. Around the pit, the sentiments of the others seemed to swing behind their leader. Pate was watching them.

Twenty minutes later, at the edge of the camp, Jema stood with him. He put his arms around her.

"Are you sure?" he said. "There's going to be trouble."

"I can't leave," she answered. "I know I can help. I have to talk to her."

Melody's arms were around Pate's leg. He looked down, smiled, patted her head and loosed her limbs. Then he turned and walked into the darkness carrying, Jema felt, a large part of her heart—if not the whole thing.

It was a long and restless night. Jema imagined herself reasoning with Kris, making her see things more clearly. At one point, Kris rolled over and lay silent for a time, and Jema couldn't tell if she was really asleep. Maybe Kris was rethinking her stubborn resolve. Maybe Kris wanted to speak to her but didn't know how to cross the divide.

When Jema woke the next morning, Melody was gone and the shelter was empty.

With concern for the little girl, Jema rose, dressed quickly and hurried outside. When she exited the shelter she saw Melody with the girls, gathered around the open trunk while Kris removed her mother's garments. They were laughing excitedly, like small birds on a branch. As Jema approached, Melody picked up her warrior doll and ran to embrace her. Kris looked up with a dark expression.

"We're going to have a loyalty party," Beth said. She explained that they had already eaten. Ry-Lynn was fastening an emerald wrap around her shirt and tattered pants. Someone had removed the blanket from the scorched mirror, and Ry-Lynn turned to pose before it. "I love this fabric," Dee said raising a diaphanous gown, closing her eyes and pressing it against her lips like a shroud.

They seemed to be trying to ignore the looming threat.

"We get to dance," Melody said, eyes glittering.

Jema smiled and nodded. Over Ry-Lynn's shoulder, Jema caught a glimpse of herself in the mirror, while the other arched and ogled. A woman, Jema thought, was more than a mirror could reflect. What did it matter that clothing made them feel grown up if they were still children?

Kris was seated on a log bench, royally dressed, elbows and arms shifting beneath the folds of a gold tunic. She was working on something propped against the bench, and Venus was helping. Dee joined them, and Beth. Kris paused and motioned to Ry-Lynn. They circled what looked like a man with a faceless head. A scarecrow, Jema saw. Venus was stuffing its legs with straw. Sticks emerged from the dummy's sleeves.

"I don't like him," Melody said.

"He's not real," Jema muttered.

Beth was bulging the dummy's shoulders with roroa sprays. Ry-Lynn pushed fern fronds into his middle. They were dressing him as they would a doll. Dee frilled his cuffs. Kris added a scarf and belt.

"If they don't like boys," Melody frowned, "why are they making one to have at the party?"

Jema didn't reply.

"I wish Pate could come," Melody said.

Jema swallowed her fear of hostility and worse estrangement, stepping closer, lowering herself onto the log beside Kris. She called to mind, forcibly, a moment when the two were on a bench in the Chancellor's garden singing a song together. Jema could understand the girls' need for escape. She, too, missed the carefree days they all remembered. She grabbed a fistful of grass and leaned toward the dummy.

"We could plump his rear," Jema said.

Beth laughed, and so did Venus.

Without turning, Kris cut a glance at her, a malevolent side-eye. Kris was coiled, crackling with hostility. "No one wants to hear about rear ends from you," she said.

The gathering was instantly still.

"You're being a child," Jema answered.

"Melody says you're pregnant." Kris looked at Jema's breasts as if they were fruit that had spoiled. Her disgust was mirthful, and the gibe spread to the others.

Dee whispered to Beth. Ry-Lynn made cups with her hands, smirking as she weighed invisible breasts. Jema put her arm over her bust. Her vision blurred, but she refused to give them the pleasure of seeing her wilt.

"This party," Kris said, "is a celebration of loyalty. You're not invited."

Jema was mute.

"Are you listening?" Kris said.

Despite herself, Jema nodded. And she felt it now—shame—the thing she'd been trying not to feel for so long. "You're as bad as Rangi," Jema said.

"You're a traitor and a whore," Kris shot back.

"She thinks she's better," Venus joined in.

Jema stared at the younger girl. When had their friendship ended?

"Pate pays her to do it," Ry-Lynn said.

Jema lunged at her. Ry-Lynn backed away, laughing.

"You need to move out of my hut," Kris said.

Jema shook her head, disbelieving.

"You can live in one of the shelters left by the boys," Kris said simply. "Or there's Pate. Melody can go or stay. I don't care."

Jema felt a pounding in her head. Melody gripped her, hugging her thighs. If I try to speak, Jema thought, no words will come out. She saw fear in the others' faces, and she began to sob. Melody was looking up at her, crying too.

"What you do with your life," Kris said, "doesn't matter to us."

Beth was mute. Dee looked tragic. None of them were going to speak up for her. They were leaning toward Kris to protect themselves.

Jema's tears kept coming, she couldn't stop. Under Kris' harsh eye, she retreated with Melody, backing then facing the empty shelters, stumbling toward them.

Melody whimpered, "We can go to the party, can't we?"

Jema drew shallow breaths, trying to slow her heart. She limped forward without speaking, holding the little hand in hers.

"We're girls," Melody insisted.

Jema fed her through the entrance of the shelter vacated by Rangi and crawled in behind her.

The camp's former leader had left a pillow of matted fronds behind. Jema set her head on it, curling Melody against her middle, whispering words of comfort and calm while she stroked the little girl's head.

At the end of the day, from the shelter's entrance, they saw a threesome walking through the trees. Kris was in the middle waving one of her mother's fans. She was flanked by Ry-Lynn and Dee; they, too, were holding fans. Dee's had flowers painted on it. Ry-Lynn's had a female dancer. On Kris' fan was a painting of a martyr, gaunt and naked, hanging from a tree.

5

The night of rejection was a long one. In the darkness, Jema's thoughts went to Pate and the Treehouse, to the waterfall and the Boggy Pit, and the view of the glittering maruna from the openings framed with branches. She felt like gathering her few belongings and starting through the jungle with Melody.

Then her confidence wavered. She had never felt so vulnerable, so cut off from others. It had been easy to flirt with the kind of future Pate imagined when her position with the girls was secure. But the new reality frightened her. Could the three of them survive on their own? There would be surprises, dangers, risks unforeseen. Were she and Pate ready to count only on each other?

Kris had always been fickle. They'd been best friends all their lives— But was there any reason to hope that things between them would mend? And the other girls? Would any of them remember their history with her, apart from Kris' derision? Jema couldn't muster the resolve to stay or go, so she kept her distance, gathering forbs with Melody while the others made ready for the celebration.

The girls had a new energy. They were quick to heed Kris' directives, having seen what could happen if they fell out of favor. Their slavish behavior made Jema conscious of the merits of a hermit existence. That was the reason Pate relished his estrangement, wasn't it? No one had authority over him. The thought made her love him even more, realizing how much he must have longed, when he was younger, for a life with others; knowing how far he'd moved in the opposite direction, fashioning himself as someone who preferred to make a life of his own.

But the need for closeness hadn't been forgotten. Why else would he want to be close to her? Then her thoughts got confused, remembering how much she loved it when they were naked together and the jungle was full of Caaqi's screams.

The arrangements for the party were nearing completion. Jema acceded to Melody's pleas, agreeing to remain in the camp through the festivity. Beth had made eel-fat candles and stuck them to the low limbs of trees encircling the camp. Kris had selected costumes from the trunk for each, and while she bossed the completion of the scarecrow, she sang waltzes she'd learned in the capital, so the girls could commit them to memory and they'd have music to dance to. At noon before the event was to start, the girls began to apply makeup to each other over their unwashed faces. That afternoon, Kris strapped a burned sheath and a blackened knife to her belt.

Just before the party began, Jema gave Melody permission, and she ran to be with the older girls. Jema retreated to Rangi's shelter. When the party was over, she meant to fly to Pate and take Melody with her. But sitting in the dimness, hearing the chatter, she found herself imagining the worst. Something had happened to him. He was stranded in the jungle, far from the Treehouse. He'd tried to pull an eel up the bank, and its jaws had clamped his leg. He was lying in a bed of vines, feverish, unable to move. Or he'd gone too far in his search for game and lost his bearings. Could he find his way back?

The singing began.

Jema peered out of the shelter. In the darkening jungle, the sight that met her eyes was a strange one. Amid the light from the fire and the circle of candles, the costumed girls seemed to dance on a stage. They were singing and waltzing around the pit with each other. As they moved, smoke seemed to rise from their hair. They'd used the makeup seductively. Eyes were darkened, temples streaked, lips stained and framed by penciled scowls. Fit for the wild setting.

Kris, in a red silk gown, danced with Ry-Lynn, waving her arms as she sang. The blackened knife hung from her belt and slapped her thigh. Ry-Lynn wore a sleek chemise, gunmetal gray, twirling the parasol over her shoulder. Its rotted lace had been re-topped with a shingling of leaves. Beth, in a dress covered with white sequins, waltzed with Dee. Melody cavorted with Venus, holding her warrior doll in the crook of her arm, her little face painted with an oversize grin. The scarecrow sat on the bench beside the fire, legs crossed. The girls had torn out a full-page photo of a leading man and affixed it to the dummy's featureless head.

At a shout from Kris the pairs broke, and the girls formed a line with Kris at the front. She led them around the fire, head thrown back, singing full-throated. Jema knew the song and she hummed along, imagining herself one with her sisters again. As Kris passed the dummy she turned her head, considering and rejecting him as a suitor.

Then a drumbeat sounded.

Jema's hum trailed off. Another reached her, like a tree thudding onto the jungle floor. If the girls heard it, they paid no mind.

A third drumbeat, much closer now. One of the candles fell, a flaming teardrop, and Jema realized in a moment that by being apart from the tribe, she could see what was coming.

An intruder bolted toward the firepit, throwing spectral shadows, whooping and frenzied, not at all like one of the boys. Another and another, with weapons raised, their naked bodies marked for war.

She recognized Rangi with his tattooed face, thorn necklace and his hair tied behind. He was shouting orders to the others now: Rodney barreling through the trees with a blade in his hand; Brice with a dagger and a hoop drum on his hip; Wyatt, club raised, his broad chest zagged with paint.

As the boys entered the camp, Kris came running up to stop them. The other girls were fleeing, dropping their fans, screaming and scattering. Melody was stranded and frozen, like a weaker animal cut out from the herd. Jema scrambled from the shelter calling for her, but the little girl was racing away with Venus. Jema ran after her, with Rangi and the boys approaching, drunk on kohu, shouting taunts and obscenities.

Rangi swung his machete at the scorched mirror, and the blinking shards flew in all directions. Snugg was unloading armfuls of clothing from the trunk and hurling them onto the fire. Brice added shoes and hats, and in a burst of sparks the finery blazed up, coiled round with smoke.

Jema reached Melody, screeched and swept her up. Rangi was shouting and waving his machete. At his direction, Snugg joined Rodney, and the two ransacked the girls' shelters. Wyatt found a tools cache and unloaded it quickly, filling his pack. Rangi approached the firepit now, snatched up the scarecrow and began to dance with him, dragging the dummy's feet through the fire, igniting straw and leaves.

The girls had retreated to the camp's edge. Jema was a few yards from them, holding Melody close while the boys' cries and whoops grew louder.

The dummy's pants flamed as Rangi whirled. One burning leg fell away, then the tattooed savage flung the scarecrow into the fire where it ignited with a roar, arms twisting and reaching out, crackling for help. Rangi raged at it, condemning it to the flames, while Brice gathered up the magazines and threw them onto the dummy's chest with an animal howl.

The girls had huddled in the darkness beneath a thicket of ferns, wide-eyed, speechless.

The boys gathered around their leader close to the fire, dancing and wailing, claiming the camp as their own. They couldn't see the girls, but they knew they were being watched; so they called out for the girls to join them, as if it was all just a frolic, hurling lewd suggestions into the darkness. Jema covered Melody's ears.

They all had weapons, Jema saw. Knives and pikes, clubs dangling from their belts. Seeing no response from the girls, Rangi jeered, calling them mop heads and waddlers.

"Midgets," Kris screamed back, "leeches, bed wetters—"

Rangi turned to the firepit, picked up a burning brand, pranced toward Kris' hut and tossed it inside. The hut torched, blooming into an onion of raging orange that lit up the camp.

Melody sobbed. Jema held her close.

Kris was motionless, silent, shocked. Rafts of sparks rose over the burning shelter. Would the boys torch them all? Jema could hear the gasps and bleats of the girls, sharing their fear, confusion, disbelief.

Rangi stood tattooed and glassy-eyed, grinning at the destruction. Watching him, a strange thought struck Jema— that his degeneration was linked to Kris; that as one went, so went the other. The heart has to love what it loves, Jema thought.

Rangi signaled and the drumbeat sounded. The leader set off loping through the trees, and the boys followed him single file, not like victorious marauders but like a troop in retreat. Gradually, the belligerent sounds faded into the jungle, and the quiet of the night returned.

First Kris, then Ry-Lynn, then the others stepped toward the shelters, seeing what the raiders had done. Jema followed, holding Melody close.

The hut Kris and Jema had used, where Melody had slept, was still smoking. It retained its shape, even as the last of the flames winked out: a gray onion of ash, each woven vine a filament, so vulnerable that the faintest breeze might cause its collapse. The girls gathered around it. Ry-Lynn reached out and touched the ashen structure, and it crumbled without a sound.

If we're homeless, we're ghosts, Jema thought. An image of the Treehouse rose into her mind, with Pate's face gazing through an opening framed with branches. In her heart, she called out to him.

Kris faced the firepit, staring at the heap of charred clothes. Jema saw her jaw clench. The leader's bewilderment was gone—there was rage in her eyes.

Dee stooped and began picking up fragments of mirror. Each shard was too small to reflect a body part, much less the portrait of an individual. Venus bent over the firepit, lifting a sleeve, the charred hem of a gown, looking at the remnants with empty eyes.

"What will we do," she grieved, "without our things?"

At the misery's center was Kris. The girls were hurting to please her, Jema saw. They all wanted to prove their allegiance. Kris looked at each of them, nursing their wretchedness in silence. Then she spoke Rangi's name as if it was poison.

Kris pulled her knife from its sheath and with narrowed eyes, staring at one girl and then another, began sawing off her hair with savage hacks, tossing handfuls into the firepit, where they curled and smoldered.

"Get me a coil of panghi rope," Kris ordered Beth. She removed her belt and unbuttoned her gown. As Jema watched, Kris lifted the red fabric over her head, revealing her small breasts and flat torso. As trim as Rangi, Jema thought, when he was twelve.

Beth returned with the coil of vine, and when she handed it over, Kris began wrapping her upper body with it, cinching her breasts down, binding herself tight as a mummy. The girls watched, rapt and uncomprehending.

"Tie me off in back," Kris said.

Beth did as she asked.

"I'm through looking pretty." Kris fixed on Dee and pointed.

Dee hurried away, returning a moment later with the sack full of makeup. She emptied the items onto an apron of moss by Kris' feet.

The leader knelt, and the others lowered themselves around her. With Kris' guidance, they gave each other new and frightening faces—blanched like ghosts or divided in two, crossed by dark lines, eyes skewered or circled, with lopsided leers and garish grimaces.

Kris pulled her gown back on over her bound torso and belted her knife to her waist. For the finishing stroke, Ry-Lynn raised the wire spiderweb mask to Kris' face, and with the leader's assent, tied it in place. To Jema, it seemed the ugliness hidden inside her old friend had worked its way to the surface.

"We'll attack them," Kris said.

"We'll take their things," Ry-Lynn said.

"Damn their things," Kris snarled. "I want blood." Her eyes hooded with craft. "We need straight shafts to bind blades to," she patted Ry-Lynn. "We'll use roroa roots for clubs," she patted Beth. "We'll make slings from vines and load them with rocks," she patted Dee.

All impediments to hatred were vanishing. Kris had discovered a taste for blood, and she was bringing the others along. Or perhaps Kris was only revealing what Jema had never been able to see. Like the actresses in the magazines, each of the girls had been playing a part. Their false fronts were stripped away now, and the grotesque makeup was giving access to their real natures.

Jema knew with sudden clarity that Pate was her future. She was finished here.

She knelt and put her lips to Melody's ear. "We have to leave."

Melody faced her, and Jema saw in her eyes an understanding of what that meant. The little girl could feel the severity of the separation and the pain it would bring.

Melody bowed her head. Then, on her own, she stepped toward the girls with the warrior doll under her arm. When she reached Venus, Melody moved the doll's chin and made it laugh. Then she held it out.

"I don't want your doll," Venus said.

"He'll be sad without you and the big girls," Melody said.

As Venus took the tatty warrior, Kris faced Jema. "You're

despised by us," Kris said matter-of-factly. Then she knelt and began to draw in the dirt with a blackened twig, discussing the details of the attack on the boys.

"We can smear maruna paste on our arms and legs," Dee said. Her eyes were surrounded by white rings, looking no longer human but instead like some startled animal.

Jema turned and walked away with Melody beside her. Her legs shook, but she didn't look back.

A full moon lit the trail, but Jema's pace was cautious.

"I'm glad you're with me." She squeezed Melody's hand.

"Are you sad?"

"I am."

"I love Pate," Melody said.

"I do too," Jema smiled.

Melody yawned. "I'm tired."

"Shall we stop to rest?"

And because they were both exhausted, that's what they did. Melody curled on a bed of dry moss. Jema stretched on her side. Sleep came, and time passed. A little or a lot—it was hard to tell. A rustling woke Jema.

She parted her lids and rubbed her eyes. She sat up slowly, peering to one side and the other. Melody lay sleeping beside her. The light was spectral—moonglow through a veil, or the first light of dawn before the sun had risen. There was so much fog that it seemed the jungle was atomizing around them. Water pebbled the leaves and trickled down the stems.

Rustling, close by.

Caaqi was ten feet away, hopping down a slope piled with leaf litter. He had his back to her and seemed not to know she was there. As she watched, he hunched his shoulders and sprawled his wings, folding them against his body like a man slipping into a dinner jacket.

Then Caaqi turned to face her. His beak opened, and a ringing alert emerged like the *ting* of a crystal bell.

What's happened to you? he seemed to say.

Was it possible he didn't know?

Jema did her best to explain how the conflicts between the boys and girls had mounted, how her love for Pate had somehow led to the loss of her best friend, how she'd been expelled from the girls' tribe and how painful that had been. Caaqi cocked his head, closed one eye and focused the other on her. She couldn't tell what he was thinking. The great parrot had many thoughts, she knew, and many voices; just when you imagined you'd heard them all, a new one sounded.

She told him about the girls' vanity and their youthful pride, and Caaqi gargled. She lamented her helplessness, and he ticked like a clock, marking time. When she described Rangi's descent, he opened his beak and made a rasping noise, like the Governor in an angry moment. Caaqi understood how hard all of this was for her, Jema thought, and how little able she'd been to affect the grim course of events.

He flapped his wings and rose, hovering two feet from the ground, batting the air at her front and face. Then he settled himself on her shoulder. Jema felt his sharp claws digging in.

Who do you think you are? the great parrot asked.

He put his beak against her cheekbone and peered into her eye. The spokes of the zodiac turned, and Caaqi's stars appeared.

I was the nice one, she said. *The one everyone liked.*

The great parrot bit the air by her nose and pecked a leaf from her cheek. A mocking whistle, a peevish sound—a sound of contempt, as if he cared nothing for nice behavior.

Who are you really? Caaqi asked.

He scooped his beak and threw his head back, like he was drinking water from a pool. *Really,* he whispered.

His voice sounded so close, she heard it inside her.

What are you telling me? Jema pleaded, listening with all her being.

Caaqi touched her hair with his beak, then he ran the sharp tip through it, sleeking, aligning.

My girl. A needed end, a vital beginning.

What was he saying?

Beautiful, wild. Naked, alone. Despair, salvation— There's a woman inside you.

A woman? What was he saying?

Can you see her? Caaqi hissed.

And Jema could. She could. That new self appeared before her, the self she'd seen in a dream before the fire destroyed her home—the luminous self she barely knew, fountaining into her body, glittering like Caaqi's stars.

Her old idea, Jema knew all at once— It was wrong. She was never the nice, attractive, pleasing person she'd imagined. She'd been weak and foolish, entrained by others. For the first time in her life, she could see who she really was. That's why Caaqi had come.

Jema raised her hand and touched his eyelid, his golden cheek, his black beak and soft chin. When she touched his crown, he rolled it beneath her finger.

Then Caaqi shrieked. Jema felt his wing clap her cheek, his claws dug into her shoulder; and the wild head, beak gaping, leaned out and frightened her with its frenzy.

Peace is precious, the Great Caaqi said, *but there are times when it cannot be had at any price.*

Jema remembered the night she'd passed through the gate on the way to Hunu's hut. She was passing through another gate now, and she wondered how many more there might be before she got to wherever she was going.

The claws let go, the chocolate wings waved and Caaqi lifted off. He rose, silhouetted against the glow of first light, banking sharply before her, dawn streaming through his scarlet fingers.

It was midmorning when they reached the Boggy Pit. The banks on either side of the river sparkled with dew and silence. The sun-warmed bark filled the air with a scent like chocolate.

Jema led Melody up the slope and around the uplifted root wheel of the giant roroa. When they reached the Pit's rim and looked down, her heart sank.

"No eels," Melody said.

"Don't worry," Jema reassured her. "He's fishing elsewhere."

As they approached the maruna thickets, they quickened their steps. Melody loved to play with the leaves. The trail led through the shrubs, and she reached out to touch a branch cloaked in shadow. Jema did too. The leaf spines flickered, sensing their presence.

Then the Treehouse came into view. "There's no place better than this," Jema sighed. With a leaping heart, she tightened her grip on Melody and hurried up the slope, expecting the odor of burning wood. But the air was clear.

Cast leaves littered the roroa footings, swollen vines crossed the Treehouse carriage. Melody let go of Jema's hand, ran to the hanging ladder and started up. Jema watched for some sign of Pate above. The little girl disappeared at the top.

Jema gripped the ladder and climbed toward her future with trembling hands. A moment later, Melody shouted, "He's not here," and her troubled face rose over the railing. Jema joined her inside, and they set about sweeping leaves from the floors, restuffing the pallets, dusting window frames and shelling clack nuts. At sundown, they heard the deck posts creak, and when they stepped outside and looked down, they saw Pate ascending.

They might have set the time and place long before. They embraced each other with the deepest and surest affection. When Pate kissed her, with all that had happened, Jema's eyes flooded. She could smell the woodsmoke in his hair, the sap of trees on his chest, the salt of his sweat, where the sun burnt his skin—everything he's done, she thought, everywhere he's been. Melody laughed at their knees.

Pate gripped Jema's shoulders, putting enough space between them to study her. He didn't look the way she remembered. His face had more lines, his brow and jaw were more gaunt. And his frame seemed larger, more muscled, with a broader chest and a straighter back. He wore a kilt of leaves and vine.

Pate was her blessing, she thought. There was Melody, and there would be at least one more. The Treehouse was her home. What reason would she ever have to leave?

"Were you hunting?" she asked.

He smiled. "You were worried about me."

"I was," she said, and she described what had happened the previous night.

Pate listened, his brow rumpled with dismay. "Was anyone hurt?"

"No," Jema said, "they just tore up the camp. But Kris is going to strike back."

"They were mean to us," Melody said.

"She's lost her senses," Jema sighed. "She wants blood. If she has her way, someone will get hurt."

Pate nodded, fears confirmed. "They're fools," he said. "I'm sorry I kept them alive." His contempt spoke an orphan's estrangement.

It was easy for him to imagine a life apart. A life of love and striving in the heart of the jungle. Jema closed her eyes. She wanted that too. Then, as if to shatter the fantasy, Caaqi's words sounded in her mind. *There are times when peace cannot be had at any price.* The burning villa, her love for Pate, the wilds, the Treehouse, the warring tribes— This was more than a blind stumble into an unknown future.

"They're not fools," she said, meeting Pate's gaze. "We need to reach the boys before Kris and the girls do. To stop them from destroying each other."

They left Melody at the Treehouse with strict instructions and set out for the boys' encampment. The sky was clear, and the blue-silver moon lit the way. They followed a path Pate had cut, moving as quickly as they could.

"I wasn't hunting," he volunteered.

Jema nodded. "The Pit was empty."

"I've been exploring," Pate said, "farther west. Following Caaqi."

She was silent.

"He's leading me deeper," Pate went on. "There are beetles that hiss, lizards that fly. Wingless birds, taller than a man. Pools with red salamanders and blue frogs. As blue as your eyes." He held the spear in his hand. The cannibal blade glinted. Its binding was darkened by blood. He's like an animal, Jema thought, and he's gotten wilder.

"I feed him mangos," Pate said.

"He was with me this morning," Jema told him. "He spoke to me."

"What did he say?"

"'Who do you think you are?'" she replied.

"What was your answer?"

For a half-dozen paces, Jema was silent. And then she let her thoughts loose, tentative as they were. "I'm strong. I'm independent. I say what I think. I'm closest to you, but I'm not like you. I'm more connected to others."

The moon shone above, the herbs crushed underfoot.

"How does that sound?" she asked.

"I can see that in you," Pate replied.

Jema waited.

"Caaqi knows things we never will," Pate said. "He dwells in places no human has been. He lives with creatures we've never seen, creatures that think and feel mysterious things."

"He acts like he has a future in mind for us," Jema said.

Pate slowed and faced her.

"But I don't know what that is," she said.

"While you were washing, Melody asked me, 'Who is Caaqi?'"

Jema was stunned. "What did you tell her?"

"'He's a parrot,'" Pate replied. "'A handsome one.' You know what she said? 'He talks to me. He knows who I am.'"

149

As close as she was to Melody, Jema thought, she hadn't suspected. A little girl— Caaqi could be saying things that would change her life, and who would know?

"I wonder if he's speaking to Rangi and Kris," Pate said.

Jema stared at him. Was it possible? What could Caaqi be saying to them? Was he rousing the kids to war? What reason would he have to do something like that?

The slope had grown steeper. They were rising to a prominence now. As Jema followed Pate onto the height, he put his hand on her shoulder and eased her down.

They knelt behind a line of boulders, catching their breath, looking down at the boys' encampment. In a notch between hillocks, Jema could see the Royal Express parked on the terminus of its winding track. Not far from the loco, the slope had washed out, leaving the rails hanging in space. Past that, the track edged a cliff and disappeared into an egg-shaped tunnel with bricked wing walls on either side.

"Look who's here," Pate muttered.

When Jema followed his gaze, she saw Caaqi's silhouette perched on a rock twenty strides away. He wasn't looking at them. He was fixed on a forested incline above the encampment.

Pate pointed.

On the incline, Jema saw a band of glowing skeletons floating through a mosaic of leafy sprays. The girls, with maruna paste on their arms and legs, were approaching a creek above the boys' camp. Moonlight varnished their clubs and lances.

Caaqi clacked his beak and lifted both wings with an impending air.

"They're going to slaughter them in their sleep," Jema said.

"If we wake the boys—"

"We can't let them die," Jema said. And with that, she stood and screamed as loud as she could. Pate joined in, hollering and calling the boys' names.

At the noise, the skeletons slowed. Jema saw Kris at the front, lance in hand, looking for the source of the clamor. Pate was rising, pointing at Rangi below.

The leader was on his feet, joining his shouts to theirs, rousing the boys. He could see the glowing ghosts through the trees. A mournful sound rose from the girls now, a wavering moan that raised the hairs on Jema's neck.

Boys were grabbing their blades, gathering around Rangi. On the incline across the stream, Jema spotted Ry-Lynn and Beth. An instant later, Kris cried out and the girls charged, hurtling down, crossing the stream, racing forward with weapons raised.

A rasping sound, like a hoarse laugh. Jema heard a flapping.

When she looked, Caaqi was off his perch, swooping toward the combatants, shrieking madly.

In the open now, lit by the moon, the girls' painted faces were frightful; their party dresses were flying, caped and scarved, ripped to rags; the boys still bore their markings from the recent raid. Kin of those, Jema thought, who'd haunted the jungle in ages past, attacking each other at every chance, lopping off limbs while the Great Caaqi swooped among them.

Snugg screamed and fell. Was it Dee who'd struck him? An agonized groan, then Jema heard him pleading for mercy. Kris was swinging her lance, headed straight for Rangi. The boys around him scattered, yelping at each other, hunched like animals springing through the trees. The girls charged after them, shrilling like ghosts, Venus among them with the warrior doll bound to her waist. His head bobbed, the mechanical laugh sounding a jarring commentary.

Caaqi flew over the melee, whistling and shrieking—a furious sound, equal parts frenzy and scorn—as if he despised them all but was enjoying the rout immensely.

"Come on," Pate said, hurling himself over the brink and down the slope, spear held high.

Jema descended behind him. Kris had reached Rangi, she saw. And she saw Kris swing—the lance flashed, and the tattooed boy doubled over.

The others were fleeing up the slope, approaching. Jema could hear the boys panting, their curses and gasps. One passed close—was it Wyatt? Like a leaf in a storm, he whirled aside. Rangi was down on his knees, blood leaking from his middle. Kris loomed over him with her lance raised. As she swung, Rangi sprang. He had a vine in his hands, and when he caught Kris' neck with it, she quivered and let go of her weapon.

A violent thrashing in a nearby thicket. Pate halted, and Snugg stumbled into him, half running, half crawling, one hand tucked under his arm. At the contact, Snugg yowled with pain, and when Pate tried to help him up, he warbled with terror. "It's me," Pate said.

Jema was at Snugg's side, but there was no recognition. He was snarling, trying to wriggle away. When Pate grabbed his ankles, Snugg went limp and curled into a ball.

Jema knelt. Snugg's hair was matted with duff. "Careful," Pate said. In the moonlight, Snugg was monstrous in his malice and fear. He lunged, snapping at Jema like a wild dog. His teeth sank into her wrist.

Pate put his knees on Snugg's chest, but he wouldn't let go, so Pate drove his fist at Snugg's head. Jema felt the teeth loosen, and Snugg's head fell back.

Pate picked him up, and with the boy limp in his arms he carried him toward the encampment's center. Rodney stood at the outskirts, watching. And so did Beth, soundless now, apprehensive, face glowing with maruna paste, her sequined dress torn and muddy.

Rangi had made Kris his prisoner. He'd torn off her wire mask and cleansed her face with dirt. She lay on the ground before him, ankles and wrists bound tightly with vines, a fistful of leaves in her mouth. Kris was still wearing her red gown, Jema saw, but Rangi had removed the belt and blade. The girls were backing away, fearful now. And the boys, stirred by Rangi's triumph, were venturing forward, returning to the side of their leader.

153

Pate put Snugg down, and as he straightened himself, he met Rangi's gaze. Jema saw a tattooed native wearing a crown of twigs, with blood in his eyes, hot as the blood that rilled from his belly. And when she looked at Rangi's captive, Kris was seething with hatred.

They're lost, Jema thought.

She felt it from the top of her head to the pit of her groin. In some afterlife, perhaps, her old playmates might learn to live with each other. Here, in the jungle, there would never be peace.

Caaqi shrieked. Pate flinched, but none of the others seemed to hear him.

Jema looked up to see the great parrot circling.

Caaqi shrieked again and swooped, heading toward the Royal Express.

Then, strangely, as if an idea had just entered his head, Rangi turned in that same direction.

6

angi and Wyatt escorted Kris up the slope, with the other boys following single file. They had loosened the vines around Kris' legs so she could walk, but her wrists were still bound and Rangi pushed her roughly. In the cold moonlight, the boys' movements had a fateful, emotionless quality. Their march was precise, their expressions icy, very unlike the previous night. Each had an ugly weapon. Only Kris' stumbling seemed human, and each time she fell they pulled her back to her feet.

They were headed uphill, Jema saw, toward the track and the Royal Express. She and Pate followed at a safe distance, with the girls behind them. Pate wore a dogged grimace. Snugg, limping, arm bloody, turned and smirked at her. Rangi's rule, it seemed, had disabled Rodney as his protector; and that had worked a monstrous change.

Rangi strode boldly, without hesitation. The machete in his hand was blackened now, but the edge was gleaming, freshened by use. The moon lit his crown of twigs and the necklace of thorns, and Jema could see his tattoo clearly. A wide grin swallowed his cheeks and chin, and a string of circlets hung from each eye—tears or bubbles or pocks full to bursting.

The moon stuttered as a cloud crossed it, then its disk was streaked with blue diagonals. The air around Jema was clear, but the rain was approaching.

Kris was led to the passenger car. When they reached it, Rangi hugged her. For a moment, it seemed like a lover's embrace and the end Kris had longed for. Then Wyatt grabbed her legs, and the two boys were carrying her up the steel grate steps, dropping her on a seat and refastening the ankle bindings. Wyatt remained in the car. Rangi leaped to the ground and hurried forward.

"What are they doing?" Jema whispered.

Pate shook his head.

Rodney, wearing a pot upside down for a hat, was stoking the firebox; it glowed orange and gold, lighting his resolute features. Rangi boarded the loco and took the controls from Brice.

The door of the passenger car was open. Jema could hear Kris groaning and sobbing through the wad of leaves. Get on your feet, she thought. Throw yourself free. But the girls' leader was helpless, and the train was beginning to move.

Pate spurred himself, racing up the slope. He reached the tracks, got his hand on the steps of the Royal Express, running alongside it faster than Jema thought a person could run. The train rounded a curve, picking up speed, and Pate lost his grip, cartwheeling to the side and into the brush.

The train pulled away. Jema could hear the boys' howls. She was hurrying forward, looking for where Pate had fallen. She spotted him crawling back up the embankment, fighting vines and saplings. A ribbon of blood glittered on his brow. He reached her, grabbed her hand, and without a word they continued beside the tracks, racing after the train together. The girls were following behind.

Where was Rangi headed? What could they do if they caught up with them? Jema saw the uncertainty in Pate's eyes. Specks of rain were prickling her face. Beyond the loco, the tunnel entrance appeared like a black egg, its edges rimmed with moonlight. The train was picking up speed, and she could feel the vibration tingling her soles, climbing her shins. The raindrops were growing in size. They stung when they hit; then all at once they were large as marbles, striking her face, thumping her skull. She could see the drops falling beside them, smacking the fern fronds.

As the train barreled into the tunnel, thunder shook the forest. A sizzle close by, then a sky-split of lightning. The ground quaked and a burnt-metal stench filled the air, mixed with the resinous scent of torn tree-flesh and the harsh mint of a crown blown apart. The speeding train emerged from the tunnel's far end. Then rumbling, rumbling, another bolt. And in the sudden illumination, Jema saw Caaqi descending through the waving boughs and the slanting downpour. The great parrot flared his wings and landed on the loco's roof.

The rain came in sheets and folded slashes; the thunder boomed and lightning branched again and again, so it seemed the train moved in leaps, as if it hadn't been fashioned by men but was rather a magical presence haunting their lives.

Who is he? Jema thought. What did Rangi want of them, their would-be chief, the friend of their youth? Though she could see the loco's smoke curdling back, and the rails trembled and sang to her feet; though she could hear the boys' shouts and the shriek of the wheels on rain-slick tracks; though she could see the rocking passenger car and the flowering of sparks at every curve— None of this seemed the least bit real.

What they chased, Jema thought, was a wicked and ghostly purging—a discharge, a banishment, an eviction of themselves.

Pate was charging forward, shoulders bowed, head down. Sodden and bedraggled, mud squishing beneath them, they raced after the mad train together as the lightning flashed and the loco drummed the jungle around them.

The train was descending a series of switchbacks. In the staccato lighting, they could see it below. The car's paint was scabrous and peeling, its curtains shredded, the seats torn up. Through the windows, Jema saw Kris twisting, struggling to free herself while Wyatt hung on to her. Two other boys—Brice and Snugg—were running along a flat car. They reached the rear door of the passenger car, opened it and stepped inside.

They crowded Kris, coming to Wyatt's aid. The three were pulling at Kris' gown, tearing the tatters off, revealing the panghi bindings beneath. Jema shrieked, looking at Pate with horror.

He pointed, shouting. On the roof of the loco, Caaqi was dancing and waving his wings, as if he meant to fly off with Rangi and Kris and the train itself.

What was Pate saying? The sky was roaring so loud that Jema couldn't hear, she could only see his lips moving. Then out of the storm came a deafening whistle: Caaqi's scream of triumph, or the piercing scream of the train itself, echoing in the gorge as it rounded a curve and zoomed down the grade toward the trestle bridge.

The jungle was a bath of madness. Flash: through the loco's spattered windscreen, Rangi's tattooed face, monstrous, raving, like Caaqi himself. Flash: by the firebox, Rodney in shock, and in the car window, Kris' terrified face; and stooping over her—flash—Wyatt, Brice and Snugg. Then the sky went black, and it seemed to Jema the jungle was suddenly thicker. The soaked vines and spasming branches were climbing the ramps of rain. The slanting torrents made tracks, the jungle rose up them like trains on rails, and every creature aboard was mad, peering into the overgrown sky, searching for Caaqi in a darkness unending.

At the next flash, the Royal Express screamed toward the trestle, starting across the bridge. To Jema, Caaqi seemed frozen, motionless. Then the loco began to glide, losing its sparks, still touching the rails but no longer gripping, carried along by some other force.

Rangi sounded the whistle, a tinny, carnival *toot*, and above the trestle, something large moved on the slope. The trees shook like some enormous animal was bounding through them. Jema saw a gap revealing itself, a space where a giant roroa had stood. The tree was leaning, uprooted by the winds and rain. And though it started down slowly—the branches of the lesser trees parting to let it through—the giant picked up speed quickly.

It crashed onto the tracks in front of the train, bark and limbs flying, with a shroud of stripped leaves swirling above. The loco kicked sideways, and for a moment the Royal Express was no longer a train but a bird taking wing. Caaqi left the roof of the cab like a figurehead departing a sinking ship.

Jema heard Rangi shout and saw him and Rodney fall from the loco. The passenger car split open and Wyatt and Snugg appeared in the gap, diving with Kris still bound and Brice following as the car broke loose. It spun like a barrel, the flat cars jackknifing behind, while the loco tumbled end over end, and the flailing bodies fell to the earth like toy soldiers.

The thunder in Jema's ears dimmed, but the rain continued to pound and the wind blew even harder. The train lay in the ravine, crooked and sliding, still writhing like a snake dropped from Caaqi's claws.

Pate motioned, his face shiny and dripping, and Jema

followed, sliding and scrambling down the slope, skirting the brambled vines and tangled trees. In the moonlight, the ravine was steaming and hissing with fast-flowing streams. They hurried beside one until it topped its banks and pooled among uprooted trunks. Below, the wreckage of the Royal Express reflected what remained of a drowned moon. The passenger car lay on its side, panels glistening, with its center torn open. The loco smoked, the fire in the firebox glowed and *sizzed*. On the ravine's far side, Jema saw the girls in a group, descending, Ry-Lynn in the lead.

Brice was clambering out of a muddy hollow, using one arm. The other hung loose. Wyatt rose from a bed of ferns. Rodney had rolled a good distance downslope. He struggled up and limped toward Rangi, who was batting wet scrub aside, making toward Kris, his sliced middle still leaking. Snugg shouted, dragging himself and his crimped arm through a web of branches.

Rangi reached Kris, stooped over her, then straightened, saw Pate and the others approaching and called to Wyatt. The lanky boy, who alone seemed unscathed, raised his arm with a blade in his fist and began scouring the ground for other weapons. Rodney and Brice had reached Rangi, Jema saw, and the three boys were gathered around Kris, still bound and gagged, lying motionless on her side.

Rangi lifted her head. Was she dead? Brice fished the wad of leaves out of her mouth. She came to life suddenly, fanging Rangi's cheek, drawing blood. Then she twisted away, crawling, dragging her bound legs.

Wyatt cried out and raised Rangi's machete over his head. Then he was hurrying forward. Snugg was too, his bloodied arm hanging by his side.

Pate continued down the slope, and Jema followed. Wyatt reached Rangi and passed him the machete. He handed a knife to Rodney and kept a club for himself. Pate halted a hundred feet from the group. The girls were on the ravine's far side, approaching.

Kris had managed to crawl a dozen feet. Rangi closed the distance, swinging his machete from side to side. The other boys followed. When Rangi reached Kris, Jema saw him crouch beside her and grab her neck. Kris snapped at his wrist and tore it open. Rangi slapped her face and spat at her. She spat back, spraying his own blood at him.

Rangi stood and drove the butt of his weapon into Kris' middle. She groaned and doubled.

Jema clutched Pate's arm.

"Get away from her," Pate shouted.

Rangi took Pate's words as a dare. He raised his machete and began to cut off what remained of Kris' gown. She twisted in the mud, trying to kick him. Rodney faced Pate, limping toward him, dragging his foot. Jema watched him stop by a rotting log, blade raised, threatening. The side of his head was raw.

The girls halted twenty feet from Jema. She could see the fear in Ry-Lynn's eyes.

Rangi removed the last of Kris' rags and tossed them aside. Kris' body was black, ribbed and gleaming, bound with panghi vine. She cursed him and Rangi laughed. Then he raised his head, grinned at Pate and gestured to the boys, pointing at Kris.

Wyatt and Rodney picked her up.

Rangi turned his back on them and the speechless girls, and with Brice guarding their flank, the boys bore Kris away.

Pate started forward and Jema followed.

"What are you doing?" Ry-Lynn called after them.

Pate looked back. "Going with them." His shoulders were slick with rain, and in the moonlight they seemed chiseled from stone.

"Where are they taking her?" Beth asked.

Pate ignored the question, facing forward, continuing up the slope. Jema went with him.

On either side, beaten fern fronds hung like tattered flags. Over her shoulder, Jema saw the girls trudging after them. From the sky, a fresh torrent. Sheets of water shimmied and snapped in the blasts of wind. There was no point in speaking. No one would hear.

The boys carried Kris up the steep slope to the train tracks and along the rails. Rangi had some destination in mind, but there was no guessing what it was. Finally, midway up a switchback, the boys left the train tracks to follow a trail that wound through the jungle.

Jema had a hard time following Pate. His pace varied,

hurrying then lagging, trying to stay close to the boys, but not too close. Was it a trail they'd hewn? There were rocks that looked carved, culverts dug, trees coaxed into arches. Signs, Jema thought, of a vanished people. Wyatt and Rodney appeared at times, carrying the bound Kris. Rodney was dragging his foot, the side of his head dark and gummy. Kris was motionless.

In places, drapes of moss hid the path. Streams came and went, burbling and disappearing, masking the sounds of the boys' passage. For a brief time, an arrow of maruna light showed in their wake. Jema wondered how Pate could see so well in the darkness. He kept a cautious distance, but Rangi knew he was being followed. She would look up and see the tattooed leader standing on a cutbank or a fallen log, peering at them through the dripping leaves.

Had the rain ceased? Was the roof of the jungle leaking? The stars flickered like candles and disappeared. Jema wished she knew what Pate was thinking. Had she been wrong to imagine some resolution? The hatred Kris and Rangi had spawned— What could they have done, what could anyone do, to bring peace to the band?

At times, Ry-Lynn and the girls drew closer, and Jema could see how shaken they were. All unexpected, Venus stumbled forward, the warrior doll bound at her waist. She looked bleary, lost; she peered into Jema's eyes and grasped her hand. Shame, innocence, a plea for forgiveness— Jema wanted to cry.

Finally the sky began to pale. A creek beside them glinted blue, and its riffles were white. The leaves showed green, and the air was full of the scent of bushes battered and thrashed. The rain had stopped, but the cold dawn left Jema shivering. Her clothes were soaked.

On a slope above the creek, the boys appeared, moving in a line with Rangi in front. Wyatt and Rodney still carried the motionless Kris. Her struggles had ended, Jema thought, along with her snipes.

A whistling came from the creek's border: a morning breeze, passing over the hollow tops of some singing reeds. Harmonies rose from their varying lengths, and they brushed together with an age-old rhythm.

The boys were approaching a ring of trees—a circle of tall roroas.

What was this place, Jema wondered. And Pate was wondering too, gazing at the perfect Ring, imagining what pruning or planting might have created it. Imagining the chiefs and the native hands, and the purpose to which they might have put it.

Rangi halted and turned. Why had he brought Kris here? He faced Pate. His eyes met Jema's, then shifted to the tribe of girls at their rear. What was he thinking? He didn't seem bothered by their proximity. He seemed half-amused, excited even.

At his direction, Wyatt and Rodney carried Kris to the Ring's perimeter and lay her in a bed of ferns before a tree. Wyatt untied her wrists and raised her. Then he drew his blade and began to cut off the binding of panghi vines, exposing her naked body. Jema could see Kris' narrow chest rising and falling. She was alive and conscious, but her eyes were closed and her lips were sealed. What was she thinking?

When the panghi vines had been removed, Rangi gave fresh orders. Wyatt and Rodney backed Kris against the trunk and used the vines to bind her to it. Rangi motioned to Brice, and he knelt at Kris' feet. He spread her legs and used vines to anchor her ankles to rocks on either side.

Jema knew now what Rangi intended. And so did Pate.

He glanced at her and crept forward, the spear with the cannibal blade in his hand, ascending the creek bank.

Jema followed, and after a pause, the girls did too. Ry-Lynn's steps were halting. Dee frowned. Venus was wide-eyed, the last to move.

Kris remained silent, head bowed; retreating, it seemed, to some interior refuge.

When the boys were done binding Kris, Rangi stepped before her and planted his machete in the soil. In the morning light, his tattooed grin and bubble-lined cheeks looked tragic. His long hair was tangled, greasy and stuck with leaves. The rip in his belly had jelled black, and his legs were burnished, freckled with dirt. He faced the group and spread his arms with a welcoming laugh. It was as if they had come for some jungle amusement.

"Go on," Rangi ordered the boys.

They loosened their kilts of leaves and let them fall. None of them looked enthusiastic.

"They'll all have a turn," Rangi said.

Pate was twenty feet from the Ring. Jema stepped beside

him. Behind them, plants rustled as the girls drew closer. The boys stood staring at them. Rangi was silent, posing. The trunks of the Ring reflected the rising sun. The tension was deadly. Who could divide play from bloodshed now?

The tattooed face turned to Kris. "You're just like us," Rangi said. "Aren't you. Not high-bred—oh no. You were born for the jungle."

Kris opened her eyes, lifting her chin with contempt. "You're the cannibal."

"Boys," Rangi laughed, "build a fire at her feet. I'm going to cook her and eat her." He looked down the slope, finding Dee and Venus. "They'll all be our food."

Jema watched and waited. None of the boys moved to gather wood.

Rangi turned back to Kris. "I'm not going to roast her whole. I'll cut off her fingers and her fine little ears, and eat them while she watches."

Pate took a step forward. Jema moved with him. Rangi was amusing himself, trying to frighten them. And he was succeeding, frightening the girls and frightening Kris. But being frightened didn't seal her lips.

"Every bite of me," she said, "will be poison."

Rangi pulled his machete from the ground. "The poison's in your head. It's easy enough to remove it."

Venus whimpered, hugging the warrior doll. Beth called out to Brice.

Pate's lips were rigid. He took another step forward. Jema followed.

"Stop," Beth cried. "Please stop!"

"You don't have the nerve," Kris dared Rangi. "Not for sex or hunting or anything else."

Why was she goading him? Jema wished Rangi would put the machete down. He was a different person with it in his hands. Couldn't Kris see that?

Rangi just laughed. He's crazy, Jema thought, and her fear was all at once intense. Not for herself or the others, but for Melody and the child she was carrying inside her.

Kris sneered at the boys. "Worms," she said with disgust.

Wyatt stiffened. Snugg grunted. Rodney spit. Like a child, Rangi skipped toward Kris, swinging the machete in a slow circle above his head. The blade was sharp, but he was playing, Jema thought. He would cut Kris free, and the show would be over.

But Pate had a different idea. He marched toward Rangi, spear raised. And Jema went with him.

Rangi was whirling, once, twice—the honed blade made a sickening hiss. Time was a loco, hurtling down, and no one was in the cab putting sand on the rails. A rooster tail of sparks from the wheels, a deafening screech as it whizzed round a curve—

Rangi put his strength into the swing, riding the current of his final whirl—

And the machete blade severed Kris' head completely.

It landed ten feet away, mouth open, surprised, eyes still seeing.

The ground seemed to shake beneath Jema. As she watched, Kris' body turned into a vase with scarlet blooms, twin bunches of them—fountains that splattered the ground at her feet.

The tattooed savage was crowing—a powerful swing, a perfect cut—

Jema was gasping, the Ring turning before her like the bars of a cage—

And now Rangi, too, was fountaining blood, though the tragic head was still attached.

Rangi lifted his hands to his throat as if he meant to remove his necklace of thorns. He tried to speak, but only a gurgle emerged. Then he was stumbling, eyes wide, realizing what had happened, wishing to somehow undo the damage.

He fell to his knees pitching forward, his head not far from Kris', struggling to speak, his face toward hers as if he meant certain words for her ear, as if he had something important to tell her.

Jema shuddered, imagining what that might be.

Laughter reached her, droll and mechanical. Venus, shocked and staring, had fallen to her knees, and the doll's chin had dropped. And now Jema realized that it was she herself standing over Rangi, and the spear with the cannibal blade was in her hand. Pate took it from her and, while she watched, he drove the blade into Rangi's chest, impaling his heart.

169

The headless figure lashed to the tree twitched and relaxed, slumping. It seemed some awful desire had been finally released. Pate drew the spear out, and it came with a welling of blood that made the blade dance like something alive. As Pate raised it, Jema saw the two chocolate feathers attached to the haft.

The tattooed boy wasn't still. A wet sound rose from his ragged windpipe, wet and croaking. A strange sound, arresting, knowing.

Jema looked up.

Caaqi was above them, perched in the crown of the tree Kris had been bound to. Solemn he was, wings folded, eyes peering down.

He'd been there all along, Jema thought. A specter of doom or an angel of mercy. Or a judge, perhaps, deciding the fate of a criminal.

Pate's head was bowed, but it seemed he could see the great parrot without having to look. Did any of the others know he was there? Jema scanned the group and saw that they didn't. Dee had fainted into Ry-Lynn's arms. Venus was wailing, the doll now mute. Snugg faced Rodney, sharing his shock.

Pate gripped the spear, not yet owning the deed.

In her head, Jema could hear Caaqi speaking.

Rangi, my boy, the great parrot said, sounding tender and sad.

Jema could feel his affection.

Look what you've done. Caaqi seemed disappointed.

Then he gave a low *chuck* of irony and amusement.

Always the wild one, weren't you.

Now Jema heard pride. As if Caaqi approved of Rangi's brutish command, his stinging mirth and unending cruelty—

Is it over for you? Caaqi said.

The great parrot lifted his wings and rose from his perch. He hovered on batting wings, turning his gaze on Jema.

Who are you now? he said, and he sounded pleased.

Jema looked at Pate, but he seemed as confused as she was. He was eyeing the two dead leaders as if he could not understand how Rangi's corpse had come to be lying at his feet, or why Kris' head had been detached from her body.

Overhead, Caaqi banked. He was flying in circles. Pate raised his head, hearing the beats, watching the wing strokes of red and gold. When he turned to her, Jema wrapped her arms around him. He had never looked lonelier, and she was in that loneliness with him, feeling an estrangement from others that might never heal. As close as she was now to the grisly remains, she could smell Kris and Rangi's mingled blood—a warm, sour smell that stopped her breath. Was Pate smelling it too?

The two of them raised their heads, watching Caaqi's slow circles, feeling his sway. Around and around, weaving a spell— All of the children were watching him now. And what did they see? The jungle's spirit, a cannibal god? For them, he was just another bird in the forest.

Brice drew on his kilt. Rodney and Snugg replaced theirs as well, standing together ignoring the carnage, pretending they'd had nothing to do with it. Beth held a sobbing Venus. Ry-Lynn helped Dee back to her feet. Flaring her lids, Dee took deep breaths, waking it seemed from a bad dream.

This was the garden, Jema thought, in which Kris and Rangi grew; and they had all fed on the bloody fruit. Caaqi was calling now. Jema felt his command. And from Pate's silence—his acquiescence, his lack of resistance—she knew he felt it too.

In the parrot's croak, there were words—words that only she and Pate could hear: *You're my children now.*

Jema thought of the skulls woven into the roots of the trees.

A long moment of silence and averted gazes.

Then Jema stepped toward a hollow and began gathering fern fronds. After a moment, she paused and asked Brice to help. He did as she asked, while the others watched. Jema, with Brice at her side, carried armfuls of the fronds toward the corpses of Kris and Rangi, setting them down in a pile between them.

"More," Jema said, and when Brice returned to the hollow, she began to free Kris' body from its bindings. Beth stepped forward to help, and so did Pate. When Kris' body was on the ground, Pate retrieved her head, and they wrapped the reassembled Kris in fronds. Some of the others approached slowly, halting a few yards away, watching warily.

"Rodney." Jema looked up. "Help me with this."

Rodney looked at Snugg, then moved forward, dragging his wounded foot, the side of his face still gummy. He retrieved some lengths of vine, knelt by Kris' wrapped corpse and began to bind it. Venus was whimpering. With the others, a gloomy silence prevailed. While she worked, Jema thought of Melody alone in the Treehouse, feeling a responsibility to both the child and the tribe. No one seemed to have any idea what to do.

When both corpses were wrapped and bound, Jema rose and stepped toward the Ring's center. One by one, she heard the steps of others rustling the duff behind her. When she reached the center, she turned. A few of the kids were inside the Ring. Pate was still by the corpses, full to the brim; ready, it seemed, to leave the kids to their fates. But Jema wasn't going to give up on them. With a sharp look at Pate, she motioned him toward her, and she did the same to Brice and Beth.

Brice stepped toward his sister and reached for her hand. She recoiled, then softened and they walked together. Rodney was next, then Dee. Wyatt and Ry-Lynn were last, eyeing each other with abiding distrust. Jema lowered herself and the others did the same, except for Pate, who remained standing.

She scanned the group, straightening her back, letting the sun strike her front. "We're wet. We need a fire. Beth and Brice will cook a meal. For all of us."

She looked at Pate. He showed neither assent nor objection.

Wyatt was eyeing Ry-Lynn with contempt. Jema saw the disdain in her face.

"It's time to recombine," Jema said. Her tone was stern.

"Who put you in charge?" Ry-Lynn sniped.

"We're going back to our camp," Dee said, facing Ry-Lynn.

"We'll go back to ours," Rodney said.

"Ours is better," Snugg nodded.

"We're abandoning both," Jema said. "Pate and I have a better place, with a stream and a waterfall, and eels nearby."

Pate stared at her, realizing what she intended. He would have preferred, she knew, to keep their haven to themselves.

"We're not taking orders from you," Ry-Lynn said.

Pate stepped toward her, planting the butt of his spear by Ry-Lynn's knee. "You'll come with us," he told them all, "if you want to eat."

A silence fell over the Ring.

Finally Dee spoke. "What about them?" she asked, gazing at the two bound corpses.

"They're coming with us," Jema replied.

What did she mean? Pate looked puzzled. Fortunately, none of them pressed her, for Jema had nothing specific in mind. Just a nagging fear of leaving the two.

Wyatt and Rodney carried the boys' fallen leader. Ry-Lynn and Beth carried Kris. Pate led the way. Jema walked behind him, holding Venus' hand.

As they descended the trail leading back to the train

tracks, Venus whimpered and began to sob. "Oh Jema, you were always my favorite."

Jema nodded and kissed her hand, but her eyes were on Pate.

For months he had fed them all, she thought. And now, because of her, he had blood on his hands. Why should he have to bear that burden? As with all his pain and estrangement, his first instinct would be to bear it alone.

I have to take care of him too, Jema thought.

7

hey left the wrapped corpses of Rangi and Kris beside the stream, near the eel trap. Jema and Pate, with Melody between them, bedded down in the Treehouse. The others slept below in the clearing.

For Jema the night was a difficult one.

Only minutes after they lay down, Melody tugged on her arm. "I want to know."

Jema wasn't sure how to answer her. "Kris and Rangi are no longer with us," she said. What could she do but give Melody half-truths about what had happened?

She kissed the little girl's forehead, then pulled the reed blanket up over her. There was a chill that would turn to steam when the sun touched the jungle canopy, but that was hours away.

The story would have to be told, Jema knew.

Pate had fallen asleep. She reached over and touched his lips, shivering at the thought of how far they'd traveled. They had ended the feud, but they'd killed a young man, once their leader. Once their friend. Could any of them ever forget that?

She closed her eyes. Sleep might not be a cure, but it could give some relief—if sleep would come. She tried to silence her mind, but there was no escaping the questions. And for some reason, the questions about the bodies bothered her most.

It was right to carry them from the Ring of Trees. There was no way of igniting or interring the corpses. They couldn't leave them out in the open, exposed to whatever creatures happened along. But now—

What would they do with them? Burn them? Bury them? And where? How near or far should they be from the living? And from each other.

The bodies were a terrible reminder of the escalating conflicts and the grisly end.

Sonorous friendships. Gentle schooling, childhood games: Storm-the-Palace and the rest. How could those innocent doings lead to such fear and loss? She imagined Caaqi flying through the trees, and she thought about all the things he'd seen. The burnt huts and painted faces, the rage and hatred—

Who are you, Caaqi had asked. And the answer now could hardly be more upsetting. Jema was the tribe's executioner.

And what about Pate? During their return to the Treehouse, he'd said hardly a word. His eclipse troubled her deeply. Would the well-meaning boy become a man in hiding? Would he walk among others, carrying this curse, unable to share or shed it? Would the bloodshed stay with them? Could any amount of love or tenderness wash it away?

The curtain of silver descended, threaded with sunlight, crystal veins beading down. Jema stood in the knee-deep pool beneath the cascade, feeling the chill water on her naked front.

A breeze descended from the waterfall's lip as she turned. Pate, naked too, was drinking from the pool, crouched like an animal on the rim, bent over the water with his hands cupped. Melody sat nearby on the moss, plaiting blades of grass.

This was their home, Jema reminded herself.

The sun was up over the trees now as if poured from a pitcher. She stepped out of the plunge pool and began to weep. Melody hurried to her. Jema received her hug and lifted her up. Pate approached with his gaze averted. Jema could feel how troubled he was.

This is their future, she knew, with all its regrets, all its perils. The jungle's fervor and tangle. It was all more real than the Chancellor's garden. Here you could hear your heart beating and fear it might stop. Caaqi's wild temper lived in every teardrop of rain, every trembling leaf.

"We're all back together now," Melody said.

Pate put his palm on her head, and Jema could read his thoughts in his eyes.

For Melody trouble was temporary. She lived with the illusion that comes with youth, that no matter the threat, she would always be safe. And she and Pate were determined she *would* be safe, like a seed planted in a garden.

But the troubles that kept Jema from sleep— There was no escaping them. Between these two truths—the adult's and the child's, the beset and the beatific—there was a narrow space. She and Pate had to find their way through it.

As they clothed themselves, smoke rose from below. Brice and Beth were roasting eel for breakfast.

The woodpile, Jema thought, should be taller, the firepit larger. Rodney's foot had been badly injured in his fall from the train. He needed crutches, and Snugg should have bark on his wound and a sling for his arm. As they descended the vine ladder toward the makeshift camp, Jema felt the burden settling on her.

They all needed reassurance. She began to rehearse what she might say.

They had known each other all their lives. Brice and Beth were still brother and sister. Dee was sorry she'd been a burden. Rodney had always been generous, Wyatt clever, Ry-Lynn resourceful. They were together again. A family, a tribe. They must agree: there will be no recriminations. All offenses will be forgiven.

Am I the leader now? Jema wondered. If she was, they would have to believe she had some control—if not of the future, at least of the moment. Could leadership that began with a murder ever bring peace to others? Jema imagined them converging on her like wandering sleepwalkers, seeking her counsel, hoping she might be wise enough to keep at bay the horrors of the past.

She turned to Pate. "I know what we need to do with Rangi and Kris."

That evening, she called the group together. Direction was needed, Jema knew. Direction and a plan.

"We're not going back," she told them. "That was always Pate's view, and I'm with him now. I feel that surely. Whatever longing for the past I once had, it's blown away like smoke on the wind. I don't need the world my parents made. This is our life, here in the jungle.

"We must build a lodge for ourselves. A place dark enough for grief and bright enough for celebration."

And with a purpose before them, the work commenced.

After careful evaluation, a location was found not far from the Treehouse. There were three large roroas—healthy ones, in a promising configuration. Using the trees as a frame, they employed the same branch-and-vine craft that Ry-Lynn had devised for their first camp. Rodney and Wyatt built scaffolds, and they wove vines through the trunks and branches. The lodge would be three stories high, flexible and alive. Storms would pass through it.

Pate was driven, like someone haunted. He set the pace, first up in the morning and the last to stop working. His keenness and purpose challenged them all. It was a surprise to Jema: with what resolution they labored, following his example. Pate's devotion, she saw, was his way of seeking atonement.

When their bodies met, it was this Jema felt most keenly—the sadness, the loss, the need for forgiveness. As the lodge grew, a new kind of commitment grew with it. Her care for Pate, and his for her, were frequently public. It was this, the dark side of love, the search for redemption, that now lived at the heart of the tribe.

For the lodge's interior, materials were harvested from the empty camps and the wreckage of the Royal Express. From the latter, there was much to salvage. They traversed the slope, recovering iron panels and spars, splintered planks and railing. The bench seats were removed from the passenger car, along with most of the windowpanes. And the loco's stack, unbent, would carry smoke from the lodge. Or "The Chapel," as it was now called, for it would be more than a place to live. It would serve as a sign of faith in each other.

The structure was nearing completion when Jema suggested a public ceremony.

It was after the evening meal. The tribe was seated around the fire, and the flames were dying. Melody put her head in Jema's lap. Snugg yawned and stood. One by one, summoned it seemed by the gravity of the stars, they rose and made their way to the pallets.

Pate put his arm around her. Jema closed her eyes, hearing the coals crumble.

"I want to be married in front of the tribe," she said.

Pate didn't reply.

"Did you hear me?" she said.

When she raised her head and saw the tears on his cheeks, something inside her seemed to burst. It was like a slow detonation of silent fireworks. A flowering of light filled her, halting her thoughts, stopping her breath.

The Chapel's first level was a communal cooking, dining and gathering area. Above that, in spiraling fashion, on the second and third levels, were the private chambers. They shared a rosette window, spoked like a zodiac wheel. Caaqi came less often now, but when he visited he would perch there and glitter for Jema or Pate, decked with mosaics of light, acting as if the edifice had been built to honor him. Above the third story, in the tapering darkness, was a garret for private conversation or silent contemplation.

It was there that Jema told Melody.

"Pate and I are going to be married. How do you feel about that?"

Melody was delighted and expressed her hope, once again, that the child inside Jema might be a boy. The ripening was well advanced now, and all in the camp saw and knew.

Jema and Pate shared their intent with the others at dinner that night. When they'd finished, Venus came forward and hugged Jema. Rodney clapped Pate on the back and embraced him. The other boys approached, offering clumsy handshakes. "Congratulations," Wyatt said with a troubled look. Troubled about what, Jema wasn't sure.

Beth thought she would make a gown of leaves for Jema, and the next morning she produced a length of vine to measure her hips and chest. Dee volunteered to do Jema's hair before the event. Venus said she'd gather flowers for the occasion. Jema asked her to find the magenta trumpets of Caaqi's Breath.

There was no makeup left, but panghi ink could be used to line Jema's eyes, Ry-Lynn said, and her lips could be reddened with roroa pith.

Venus was happy for her, but she seemed to want Pate to be moonier than he was, influenced perhaps by the romantic ideals she'd absorbed from the magazines. "He's so serious," she said.

"He needs me," Jema explained.

Venus looked confused. "Do you need him?"

Jema nodded, seeing something in Venus' eyes she had not seen before. "I do."

The Chapel's minaret was shingled with palm fronds, as a sign of its completion. Two days later, Jema and Pate drafted their vows. They were simple enough. But Jema wanted to say more to the tribe, not about her personal hopes, but about her hopes for them all. She worked on that the following day and long into the night.

The morning of the wedding, Dee braided Jema's hair.

Jema stood in the plunge pool below the Treehouse

cascade while Dee poured water over her head. Then Dee led her to the rocky shelf and a splash of sun.

"There's color in your cheeks," Jema said.

"It's the eel, I suppose," Dee replied. The deaths of Rangi and Kris had given her a new respect for life and an acceptance of what survival meant. "I don't like the taste."

"A girl has to eat," Jema said.

When the braids were done, Dee pulled them tight and coiled them into a crown.

The sun was rising, rays wheeling through the trunks and boughs. The warmed roroa bark filled the air with the scent of chocolate.

The wedding processional wound through the marunas, descending.

At the front, Jema wore a gown of lapped leaves; Pate was bare-chested, with an eel skin cape; and Melody skipped between them. Each of the girls had a fresh-picked magenta trumpet hanging down her front. Beth took solemn steps in a low-cut bark peel bodice, the tops of her breasts flaming in the light. Rodney, at her elbow, could not look away. At the rear were Ry-Lynn and Wyatt. She walked as gracefully as a deer. He had a new gravity they were all trying to fathom.

The wedding couple, with Melody between, climbed the low hill to the Chapel portico, while the rest of the tribe circled below.

I'm a woman now, Jema thought. She felt the burden she was carrying, but her heart felt a little lighter. She imagined Melody in the jungle with others, children of the tribe, running through trees, calling to each other like wild birds.

Pate spread his arms to get their attention. His vows were first.

"Jema is the one I've always loved," he said.

How fortunate she was, Jema thought. Pate's voice, as he spoke his pledge, was the most earnest she had ever heard. And she would hear it for the rest of her life.

"I want her to be mine," he finished.

She smiled and raised her head. The light seemed richer in that moment, sliding down from above, covering her and Melody with gold. Pate was asking for her reply. She put her hand on her hip—her gown was fastened down the side with twig hasps—and drew a deep breath.

But before she could speak, she heard a flapping of wings.

Jema looked up, seeing only the sweeping rays of the sun. The flapping grew louder, approaching her ear. Amid shuttered strobes and pulses of light, a beak appeared, and a magical wing flashing scarlet and gold. He had come, of course. She and Pate were Caaqi's brood.

The parrot's black eye flashed as he landed on Pate's shoulder. Then Caaqi turned his head toward her, and she felt all his wildness, his frenzy and terror. They had killed, Caaqi knew. And they had both smelled the odor of madness.

It's time to speak, she thought. Pate was nodding to her.

186

Jema recited her vows with a firm voice, scanning the faces before her.

"I want him to be mine," she said loudly.

Caaqi was listening.

Pate embraced her and they kissed. Shouts and claps rose from the tribe, but the approbation seemed to come from a distance. Jema closed her eyes.

I will hold this kiss, she thought, until the seasons have gone all the way round and I'm another year older.

When she opened her eyes, she saw Venus crying and knew it was done.

Then Caaqi jumped onto her shoulder; and with his claw tips needling, she faced the group and summoned her words.

She had a wish, Jema said, she wanted to share: that they would remember the path they'd traveled and the mistakes they'd made, and not be naive about the challenges they were about to face. They had survived—they were natives now. But they lived in a jungle, where all that they didn't know far outweighed what little they did.

Her wish was for reason, for balance, for trust and hope. It was all so unlike who she'd been just a year before.

"We are friends and confidants," Jema told them, "brothers and sisters, husbands and wives. We're laborers in a common struggle. We aren't cannibals."

As she spoke the last phrase, Jema saw Ry-Lynn eyeing her with suspicion—the same suspicion she'd shown months before when she'd asked what Jema intended to do with Kris' body.

The day after they arrived at the Treehouse, she and Pate had dragged the corpses to the Boggy Pit. Together, they removed the bindings and peeled the ferns away.

Kris, with her open eyes, was still so present that Jema understood why people believed in ghosts. Jema grabbed Rangi by the ankles and wrestled him into the Pit. She did the same with Kris, folding her legs into a space where roots had been. Pate sat down on a log to watch. He had done all he could with these two. He hadn't the heart to go farther.

Jema retrieved Kris' head from the rim, lifting it by its tangled hair; and she bore it to Kris' frame, setting it in the muck above the ragged neck, faceup.

"That's what you want?" Pate said.

Rangi and Kris were staring at the sky.

Jema nodded. "Go ahead and secure them."

But while he was working, Jema's confidence flagged. As physically close as they were, Rangi and Kris seemed indifferent to each other.

Jema descended back into the Pit and turned Kris' head. And that was enough. Between the two now, Jema could feel a terrible tension. Kris was fixed on Rangi, and she could stare at him until they both decomposed.

On the Chapel portico, a breeze drifted past Jema's braids. She could see that Ry-Lynn's suspicion had spread. The names of Rangi and Kris were unspoken, but they seemed to echo in the uneasy pause.

"We aren't cannibals," Jema repeated. "But none of us should forget that our home is here, where the cannibals ranged. We will look for our hope between heartbeats, in the space between people. But we will not forget: the roots of these trees," she raised both hands and curled her fingers, "hold the skulls of warriors who dream of rejoining the living."

Caaqi shrieked and spread his wings.

As he left her shoulder, Jema felt the sharp line of feathers score her cheek. She followed his flight, watching him strafe the marunas and enter the trees, remembering the moment at the window of the Royal Express, when the great bird emerged from her dream.

Caaqi banked and screamed, angling between boles, cutting between sprays without trembling a leaf. Mounting a ridge, he made a swooping descent, passed through a grove and crossed a stream. He came swerving around a roroa trunk, underwings flaring. His dark beak opened, his claws reached down and he batted to a standstill, settling on a naked bough, the lowest on the tree.

Caaqi's chocolate coverts folded over his back. His head twitched and tilted, then he closed his beak and looked down.

The Boggy Pit was below him—the broad, circular hole left when a giant roroa upended. The rotting trunk and the wheel of roots were visible downslope.

Caaqi scanned the Pit's rim, where sunlight winked on the leafage. Then his black eyes irised and the zodiac opened, drinking in the sight at the Pit's center. Two teenagers lay on their backs. The boy's neck had been pierced. The girl's head had been severed, but it faced the boy's and was fixed on him with an inhuman fury.

The bodies were staked beneath a blanket of water. Handrails taken from the Royal Express had been hammered through the thighs and biceps of each, to make sure neither would wander. Secured in the Pit, they could keep Caaqi company at all seasons.

He visited in daylight and at night too, watching over Rangi and Kris as if they were children tucked in, but who wouldn't be waking.

The Pit water was oily and sour. Nothing grew there. No passing creatures hungered for those leathery hearts. It was a grim reminder for any who cared to visit.

Was Caaqi glad for the ascendance of Jema and Pate, for the unification of the divided flock? Had the deaths of the two leaders pleased him? Did he feel some pride in having arranged that? Or was he mourning their loss? It was hard to know.

He perched always at the same spot on the lowest branch, cucking, warbling and preening, eyes pinning and flaring, hatching dreams of love and terror, beauty and blood.

On this day, so clement for the tribe's celebration, a light breeze stirred his feathers.

Rich Shapero's novels dare readers with giant metaphors, magnificent obsessions and potent ideas. His casts of idealistic lovers, laboring miners, and rebellious artists all rate ideas as paramount, more important than life itself. They traverse wild landscapes and visionary realms, imagining gods who in turn imagine them. Like the seekers themselves, readers grapple with revealing truths about human potential. *Beneath Caaqi's Wings* and his previous titles—*Dreams of Delphine, The Slide That Buried Rightful, Dissolve, Island Fruit Remedy, Balcony of Fog, Rin, Tongue and Dorner, Arms from the Sea, The Hope We Seek, Too Far,* and *Wild Animus*—are available in hardcover and as ebooks. They also combine music, visual art, animation and video in the TooFar Media app. Shapero spins provocative stories for the eyes, ears, and imagination.